the christmas ornament

EVERGREEN LAKE: UNDER THE MISTLETOE

DL GALLIE

I'm days away from marrying an incredible man.

We're so close to our happily ever after, but with our big day looming, storm clouds are beginning to appear.

My groom is becoming distant, and when my best friend gives me an early Christmas present—a beautiful, one-of-a-kind, handblown Christmas ornament—I'm not ready for the *snowball effect* it's about to have on my life.

Honestly, how can one Christmas ornament send things spiraling so out of control?

According to the shopkeeper my friend purchased it from, the ornament is *enchanted*. Yes, enchanted. Supposedly, now that it's in my possession, I'll be able to look into the future and find my one true love.

I decide to play into the old lore.

Besides, it's all in good holiday fun…
Until I ask who my one true love is, and I'm met with the one man I swore I'd leave in my past: my best friend's brother.
What happens next is a series of fa-la-la-la frenzy. My fiancé leaves me at the altar, and I start to wonder … could that ornament seriously be enchanted?

Stranger things have happened…

Merry freaking Christmas to me.

The Christmas Ornament is a second chance, best friend's brother, holiday romance! It has themes of Christmas magic, and our two main characters have to bundle up tight during a snow-storm! 1-Click The Christmas Ornament today to find out what happens next!

CHRISTMAS TRAIN

WINTER TREE FARM

ICE SKATING RINK
LIPS & HIPS

EVERGREEN ROAD
SIPS ON MAIN

READ BETWEEN
THE WINES
TOWN
SQUARE

GINGERBREADS
MAIN STREET

POLICE STATION
NADINE'S
NURSERY

CHAMBER OF
COMMERCE
HANSON'S
MERCANTILE

FIRE DEPT.
LIBRARY
FAIR ROAD

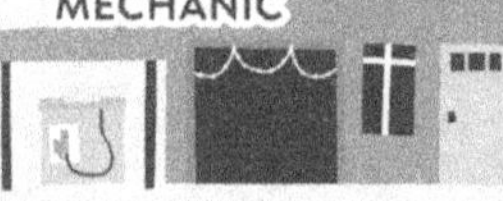

MECHANIC
CHURCH

WELCOME TO
Evergreen
LAKE

EVERGREEN LAKE INN

SKI LODGE
THIS WAY
FOR SALE
LAKE STREET
SANTA'S
CLOSET
POWDER
ROOM

EVERGREEN
PET RESCUE
THE REINDEER HOLE

LAKE SHORE DRIVE
EVERGREEN
LAKE
CHRISTMAS
FESTIVAL

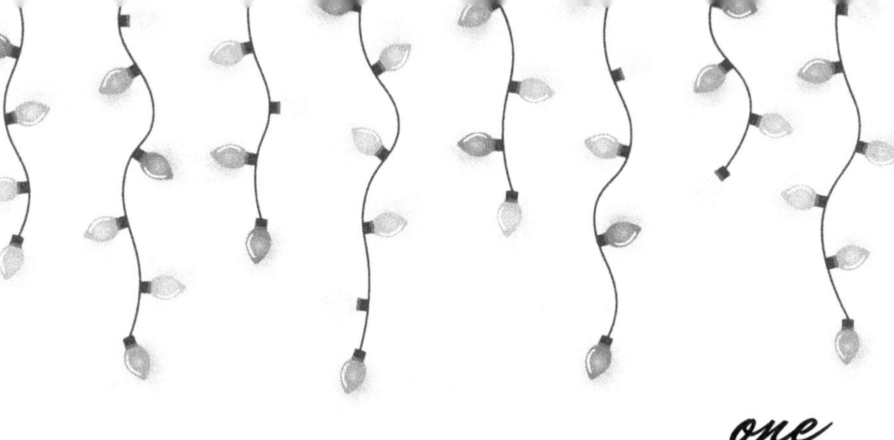

one

I'VE BEEN in the car for what feels like forever, and I still have a few hundred miles to go. I'm returning to my hometown, Evergreen Lake, Nevada, to take up the sheriff position there. I never thought I'd be moving back, but when I heard Sheriff Roberts was retiring, something compelled me to apply.

My sister, Sabrina, or Sabbi as I affectionally call her, is pissed I'm leaving because I was her go-to babysitter for when her and Eamon wanted a night out. I'd take my nieces, Monique and Cassie, for the night and the three of us would have an amazing sleepover. Uncle Maddox would fill them up on all the foods my sister never lets them have. We'd watch inappropriate movies for girls of their age and then I'd send them home on a sugar high, and sometimes with nightmares and tears. I'm still sorry for *The NeverEnding Story* incident; I totally forgot about the part with the horse. Sabbi was pissed for weeks over *that* movie choice. Now I need to clear with her beforehand what movie we are going to watch.

Packing up my apartment in the city left me feeling morose. Usually, by this time, my house would look like Santa's village had thrown up, but this year feels different. It's already the fifth and I don't have a tree up or any decorations, but that'll be the first thing I rectify when I get settled. But before I turn my home into a winter wonderland, I need to get there.

Christmas is in the air everywhere I look, and it's another slap in the face. Christmas is a magical time of year and I'm manly enough to admit, I love the holiday season. There's this shop in the city I visit every year, and I always come away with a new ornament for my tree. This year's ornament is different than what I would normally get, but I was drawn to it like a moth to a flame.

As soon as I held the delicate, glittery crystal in my hand, I knew I had to have it. As I was paying, the lady behind the counter had a knowing smile on her face. It started to give me the creeps, but as I was leaving, she called out to me. I turned to face her, and she mumbled something to me about having a magical Christmas. Nodding at her, I gave a little wave and I left, wondering what that was all about.

After stopping for a quick pee break, I grab some snacks and more coffee. With my goodies in hand, I climb back into my car and hit the road. After a few hours delay due to a freak snowstorm, I finally pass the "Welcome to Evergreen Lake" sign and a sense of calm washes over me. "Finally," I mumble. This last stretch along the lake into Evergreen Lake is always the worst. The roads are windy, and if you aren't careful, you'll crash.

Driving along the icy, windy road, I speed up a little since I'm almost there. I'm aware I'm the sheriff and I shouldn't be speeding, but I know these roads like the back of my hand. After a million hours on the road, I just want to get there. I want to put my feet up, drink a beer, and start decorating for the holidays, but when I round a corner, it all turns to shit.

There, in the middle of the road, is a fucking huge deer. Slamming the brakes on, I skid along the icy road, somehow, I manage to miss the animal, but my truck skids along the road. I spin the wheel, trying to regain control, but I overcorrect and make things worse.

It's game over.

My truck runs off the road, and I crash into a snowbank with an almighty bang. My head collides with the steering wheel, and I see stars. Don't know if I'm grateful or not that the air bag didn't detonate but either way, it's left me stranded and disoriented. I blink a few times, and my vision finally clears. "Fuck me," I groan.

Touching my head, I flinch at the forming lump and when I pull my hand back, there's red dotting my fingertips, and that's when I feel a rivulet of blood streak down the side of my face. Wiping at my head, I do nothing but smear blood everywhere.

Reaching for the ignition, I turn the key over but nothing happens. I try again and again but the engine just won't start. "For fuck's sake," I hiss, slamming my palm into the steering wheel in frustration.

Grabbing my phone, I swipe at the screen and, like my engine, nothing happens. "Great, it's dead," I groan, tossing the useless device onto the seat next to me. Craning my neck, I look around, trying to gauge how far from town I am, but it's been a while since I was here and since it's dark out, I don't know where exactly I am. There are no streetlights out here and the moon is hidden behind some clouds, I'm shrouded in darkness. In the distance, I see a cottage down by the lake, lights shining in the front windows. From memory, this area is predominately holiday homes so I'm not hopeful anyone will be home right now, but then again, they could just be security lights to give the illusion someone is home.

A chill sets in and I know I can't stay here, otherwise, I'll freeze to death—and I refuse to die because I crashed my car into an embankment due to a fucking deer. Reaching over to the passenger seat, I grab my coat and pull it on as I climb out. The wind picks up and I shiver. The evening air is fresh and has that feel like it's going to snow soon. Pulling my jacket tighter around me, I hustle across the road and down the street. Stepping onto the long driveway, I head toward the cabin and, like I predicted, it's just started to snow. Flakes fall from the sky and I smile. My smile widens when I see two cars in the driveway. Luck is on my side and relief hits that I won't be stranded by the side of the road while it's snowing.

Christmas music filters up the driveway, and I find myself grinning as Wham sings about last Christmas and giving my heart away. Then I think of *her*. I gave my heart to her a long time ago, and she's had it ever since ... even if I was a dick and walked away. Maybe this Christmas will bring a miracle and I'll get a second chance, but miracles only happen in the romance books I read. Yes, I read romance, there is more to them than just sex. I'm man enough to admit I love reading smut ... just in secret ... on my Kindle ... where no one can see what I'm reading.

Making the few final steps to the cottage, I raise my hand and knock.

two

RUBY

"OH MY GOD, Rubes. I can't believe you're getting married in just over two weeks' time," my best friend Sabrina aka Sab says. "Then you'll no longer be Ruby Olsen, you'll be Ruby Prior." She tops off my wine glass and drops down into the seat next to me by the fireplace.

Sab is here for the weekend plus a few extra days because she surprised me and arrived early for a little Sab and Ruby time, hence my midweek drinks with her. Even though I live here, we rented a cottage on the lake because it will allow us to attend the annual tree lighting but still get away for some girl time. It's my unofficial bachelorette party. Getting drunk in Vegas isn't my style, so Sab and I decided on a girls' weekend with wine, cheese, and a hot tub.

The cottage she booked has a wraparound porch with a swing out front. It's open plan inside with a large living area and a gourmet kitchen, with top-of-the-line appliances and granite countertops. There's a hot tub on the huge back deck that overlooks the lake, and just off the deck is a firepit. There's a stone path down to the lake and a private dock. I'm going to suggest we come here in the summer too so we can make use of the private dock, lake, and firepit ... without freezing our tits off. The winters here can be unbelievably cold but in saying that, today can be in the negatives and tomorrow will be twenty degrees warmer. Mother Nature can be psycho at times.

The original plan was for me to finish early on Friday. Sab is going to pick me up from my place, and then we'll head into town for the annual tree lighting before the two of us are going to hide out together at the lakefront rental for the rest of the weekend. I'm looking forward to sitting in the hot tub with my bestie, where we will drink copious amounts of wine and laugh.

Oh my God, will we laugh.

Sab and I always laugh when we're together and they say, "laughter is the best medicine" and Dr. Sab is a pro at making me chuckle. Hopefully, it will be the medicine I need to calm my inner unrest. Even though it'll just be the two of us, I cannot wait. It will be my last chance to relax before the chaos of Christmas and the final wedding prep begins.

Like seriously, who gets married just before Christmas? Ohhh, that's right, me. I'd always dreamt of having a Christmas wedding, so as soon as Joel proposed the planning began. He wanted to get married at the ski lodge—not my preference—so we booked it for the weekend before Christmas the following year. It was already August by the time he proposed, and there was no way I could arrange a wedding in four months. I may be a planner from way back but I didn't need stress like that, so we agreed to the following year, and here we are; our big day is almost here.

Sabrina has been a life saver when it came time to planning the wedding, she really is the bestest friend a girl could ask for. She and I have been best friends since the Whitworth's moved in next door when we were seven. As an only child being raised by her grandparents, after her parents were killed in a house fire when she was three, it was great to have kids nearby. She's my sister from another mister. My ride or die. There isn't one memory from my childhood that doesn't involve her.

We always joked around about me marrying her older brother, Maddox, and then we could become "real" sisters and I was always happy to go along with that plan. Her brother, Maddox Whitworth, is the most beautiful man in the world and it would have been no hard feat to marry him, but best friend's brother is so cliché … even if my romance-loving heart would love that.

She, along with her parents, were always aware of my crush on her brother, which as the years went on became an infatuation. But if she'd seen what I'd seen when I was sixteen, she'd understand. It was a Saturday afternoon in July, and I got more than I bargained for when I went upstairs to pee. I walked into the bathroom, and I saw him in nothing but his birthday suit. He'd just stepped out of the shower and was reaching for his towel. Water droplets slid down his body, it was the first time I'd seen him without a shirt on that summer, and thanks to his rigorous training at the police academy, Maddox Whitworth had abs on abs on abs. And his dick? Oh, my God—perfection. It was the first dick I saw in the flesh, and it was massive and beautiful. My little sixteen-year-old-heart fell deeper for him and my crush intensified tenfold. No other dick has ever lived up to that memory, sorry Joel. Don't get me wrong, my fiancé has a nice dick but as of late, in the lead-up to our wedding, our sex life has become *meh*. Thank God for Thumper, my trusty vibrator, but I digress, back to Maddox. He was the man of my teenage dreams and secretly, like her, I always hoped Sab and I would become sisters-in-law. That dream almost became a reality a few Christmases later. For two blissful weeks, Maddox and I snuck around together. That Christmas, he took my virginity, and my heart. I remember that night as if it were yesterday and not nine years ago. It was late and we'd both had a little too much mulled wine at the Christmas festival. One thing led to another and he popped my cherry in their garage apartment. It was magical and once wasn't enough so we kept doing it while we were both home, then real life kicked in and we went our separate ways. Sab doesn't know he was my mystery man that Christmas or that he was the one to take my V card. It was nothing more than a holiday hookup and we've never spoken about it since. In fact, I haven't seen him since Sab's wedding but now he's the new sheriff, I'm bound to run into him from time to time.

According to Sab, he's still single and is leaving a trail of broken hearts behind him. She thinks he's pining over a girl because he once let slip that he let "the one" go, but he never told her anything more about this mystery girl. I like to think it was me, but it's too late now because very soon I'm going to become Mrs. Joel Prior.

When I met Joel, he swept me off my feet and we fell in love. Just after we graduated, Joel got a job in Kingsbury Point, just across the lake from Evergreen Lake, at the Luxe Hotel there in the accounting department. It made sense for us to return to my hometown since I'd inherited my grandparents cottage. My pop, Erik Olsen, my last surviving family member, died just before I graduated. He never got to see his Reindeer—the nickname he gave me because my nose is always red like Rudolph's, even in the summer—walk across the stage and get my degree, and he won't be there to walk me down the aisle in a few weeks' time.

With Kingsbury Point being only a thirty-five minute drive around the lake, it wasn't too much of a commute for Joel, and the move back home allowed me to open my very own bookstore on Main Street. In doing so, Read Between the Wines went from being a dream of mine to a reality.

Six years later, my little store is thriving and my romance-loving heart gets to indulge each and every day. Books are a way to escape reality and book boyfriends are perfect in every way, even the douches. Sometimes I wish Joel was like the hero in my novels. I wish he'd come home from work, walk over to me, and slam me up against the wall. Devouring my mouth with his tongue, while stripping me naked, and fucking me right there in the living room.

He does deserve credit where credit is due because when he proposed it was super romantic. We were in Hawaii on vacation, staying at the Luxe resort in Lanikai Beach. He'd arranged a sunset dinner on the beach across the road, and just as the sun dipped beneath the horizon, a sign was lit and as the flames grew, it heated up the frame and the words, "Marry Me?" appeared. When I looked back to Joel, he was down on one knee with a ring. Of course I said yes, who wouldn't after a proposal like that?

As soon as we got back to Evergreen Lake, the planning for our special day began and now, sixteen months later, our wedding is nearly upon us.

The sound of Sab's voice snaps me back from my memories and I listen as Sab tells me a story about her girls, Monique and Cassie. I love those girls as if they were my own, and I cannot wait to see them in their flower girl dresses.

"You realize you created mini versions of us? Mon and Cass are just like you and me from when we were younger."

"Oh my God, you're right. I'm screwed when they become teenagers."

"At least you'll kind of be prepared."

"Thank God for wine," she states. Raising my glass, we tap them in a silent cheers.

"Your turn," Sab says, pointing to the empty wine bottle.

"I have to work tomorrow."

"Rubes, you're the boss, you can go in late."

"Well, yeah, but—"

"A girl needs to let loose every now and then and when your sister from another mister arrives early, you drink wine and eat cheese with her."

"Well, when you put it like that, how can I resist?"

"You can't, now, wine me."

Saluting her, I jump up and head into the kitchen for another bottle of wine. When I return, she's sitting there with a sheepish look on her face.

"What are you up to?" I ask, as I refill our glasses and sit back down.

"Here," she states. "Happy early birthday," Sabrina singsongs, handing me a beautifully decorated gift box.

"My birthday isn't until March," I remind her.

"Hence early. Now open it."

"Okay. Okay." Lifting the lid on the box, my eyes widen when they land on the most beautiful Christmas ornament I have ever seen. It's a handblown purple, blue, and pink star adorned with glitter. It's so delicate I'm scared I'll break it. "Sab, it's gorgeous."

"I grabbed it from this store Mad was telling me about in the city, but as soon as I saw it, I knew you needed it. The storekeeper told me it was enchanted."

"Enchanted, huh?"

"Mmmhmpf. She said the person who receives it would be able to look into their future to find their true love. It was that story that sold it for me because I knew you and your romantic heart would eat that shit up."

"Sab, I already have my true love."

"But do you?"

Her question shocks me and I pause. "Yes?" My answer is more of a question than a reply, but I do love Joel. "I love him," I tell her.

"I know you do, ignore me, but seriously, do you really love it?"

"I do, Sab, I really, really love it. It's stunning and I can't wait to put it on my tree when I get home."

"Before you do, make sure you ask it to show you your true love."

"For you, Sab, I'd do anything." Carefully, I pull out the ornament and I hold it up by the gold string, I stare at the shimmery ornament. "Okay, ornament, show me who my one true love is."

No sooner do I finish asking the ornament who my one true love is and there's a knock at the door.

three

MADDOX

KNOCK KNOCK KNOCK

My knuckles wrap on the front door, which has a gorgeous wreath full of vibrant red poinsettias, red berries, and golden baubles. A massive ribbon bow sits proudly on the wood, and from the smell, it's real and not one of those fake things from the chain stores.

The door swings open and the warmth from the cottage envelops me and my eyes widen when I see who opened the door.

"Maddox." A soft voice that haunts my dreams cuts through the frigid night air, followed by a screeching, "What the fuck are you doing here?"

"What are you two doing here?" I ask, my gaze snapping from my sister to her best friend and back to my sister again.

Ruby Olsen, aka Reindeer, is just as stunning as I remember. Her hair is a gorgeous golden-blonde and pulled up into a messy bun on top of her head. Her eyes are a shade of hazel that changes depending on the light; right now they are a combination of brown, green, and gold and they are staring intently at me. Her chest is rapidly rising, her tongue darts out and swipes across her lower lip. Lips I know are plump and soft but I need to forget that. A, she's about to get married, and B, my sister doesn't know about what went down with us that Christmas. If she knew what happened between Ruby and me, all hell would break loose because we all know, your sister's BFF is off-limits. Hence, why Rubes and I agreed to keep it a secret—then and now.

"We're having a girls' weekend," my sister says, pulling me in for a hug. "What are you doing here?"

"I'm moving back this weekend but, I, umm." I squeeze the back of my neck. "I had a little car accident—"

"Are you okay?" Reindeer interrupts. Her eyes roam over me, looking for any injuries ... or she's checking me out.

"I'm fine, Reindeer, but my truck, not so much. Can we, umm, maybe take this inside? It's colder than penguin snot out here," I tell them.

"Penguin snot, really?" my sister hisses while Ruby laughs.

"Yep, or would you prefer colder than a well digger's ass?"

"What does that even mean?" she asks.

"It means it's fucking cold. Now, you going to let me in?"

Taking a step closer, I stand under the porch light when Ruby screeches, "Oh my God, you're bleeding."

"Ohh, yeah, my head."

"Come inside and we'll get you patched up." Ever the mother hen, Ruby looks to my sister. "Get the first aid kit from the kitchen."

"Yes, boss." Sabbi salutes Ruby and she walks away from us.

Reindeer steps closer to me, and she rests one hand on my forearm while lifting the other to my forehead. Gently, she runs her finger over my hairline and down my face. My skin burns under her touch, but the moment is interrupted when Sabbi shouts, "Get the fuck inside, you're letting all the hot air out. I reckon my nipples could cut glass right about now."

Reindeer chuckles and I shake my head. That's not an image I need in my mind. Stepping inside, she guides me into the cottage after closing the door behind us. She leads me over to the dining table and gestures to the seat she pulls out for me.

Lowering into the chair, I stare up at her. She has concern etched all over her face. Lifting my hand, I rest it on her hip and squeeze. She drops her gaze to my hand, then back to my face. Again, Sabbi intervenes and she steps back from me.

Opening the first aid kit, Sabbi grabs some antiseptic solution and a gauze pad. She soaks the pad in the liquid and gently wipes it over my head wound. A hiss slips out and my sister teases me, "Is the big bad police man afraid of a little antiseptic?"

"No, you're being rough."

"Please, Mon is tougher than you when it comes to cleaning up scrapes."

We all laugh because Monique McMahon is a walking disaster. She always has a Band-Aid covering one of her many injuries; she's the complete opposite of her sister. Cassie is a bookworm and as she tells us, "You can't get hurt from a book." Well, except for that one time when Monique threw a book at Cassie to prove that you can, in fact, be injured by books.

"You were speeding, weren't you?" my sister unhelpfully asks as she applies a Band-Aid to the cut on my forehead. She pulls off the rubber gloves she slipped on and begins to clean up the mess. She returns with a glass of water and two headache pills. She drops the pills into my palm and hands me the water. Swallowing back the pills, I stand up and look about the living area.

"I'm not you; I do not speed." That comment earns me a bird flip from my sister, and I flip her right back. "Nice digs," I voice.

"It'll do for the weekend," Sabbi says. "I'm still pissed Mom and Dad sold our house on the lake here when they retired. Had they said something, I would have bought it as a holiday home. I couldn't live here full time—"

"You're such a city girl now," I tease her.

"Yes, yes I am but so many memories were made in that house."

"So many," I echo, my eyes locked on Reindeer's and I can tell she's remembering what I'm remembering. "You got a charger?" I ask.

Sabbi holds her hand out for my phone, and I drop the device into her waiting palm. She walks over to the desk by the window that overlooks the back deck and plugs it in for me.

"Are you sure you're okay?" Ruby asks.

"I'm fine. There was a fucking huge deer in the middle of the road. I overcorrected and ran into the embankment just up the road."

"That's Murray," she tells me. "He's been causing mischief for years now. One of these days he's going to get someone killed."

"Why doesn't Game and Parks just move it on?"

"They've tried, but Murray the Mule Deer always returns." She gets a wistful look on her face. "Personally, I think he has a secret girlfriend here and that's why he keeps coming back."

"Well, this town is like a boomerang, people and deer, it seems, always come back," I offer.

"Not me," Sabbi singsongs, handing me a glass of red wine. "I'll come back to visit my two favorite people in the world, but I cannot see myself ever living here full time." She takes a sip of her wine. "To be honest, I'm not shocked you're moving back."

"Yeah, me neither," I reply with a nod. "As soon as I heard Sheriff Roberts was retiring, I knew I'd be returning to Evergreen Lake. Once I mentioned I was interested, one thing led to another and here I am, the new sheriff in town."

"Well, as much as I hate that I'm losing the best babysitter I have ever had, I'm glad you're following your dreams." My sister pauses and smiles. "I remember you telling me when we were kids that one day you'd be the sheriff here, and look, at the ripe old age of thirty-two, you're childhood dream has come to fruition."

"Look at you using big words." She flips me the bird again and takes a seat next to Ruby—who is staring intently at her phone and worrying her lip between her teeth.

"Still no answer?" Sabbi asks Ruby.

She shakes her head. "Nope, but his phone has been acting up."

"Who's missing?" I ask.

"No one is missing," Ruby tells me, "but I haven't heard from Joel since I left a voicemail to say I was coming to have dinner with Sab."

"Is that out of the norm?" Again, she shakes her head. "Do you want me to call the station, see what I can do?" Her head moves side to side, again. For someone who is getting married in a few weeks' time, she seems, I don't know, not how a bride-to-be should be acting. I remember when Sabbi was about to marry Eamon, she was glowing and high on life, but Reindeer? Well, she's just Reindeer.

"No, it's fine, but thank you. I'm sure he'll be in touch before he goes to bed tonight."

"Won't you see him before you go to bed?"

"We, umm, don't live together."

"How does that work if you're getting married soon?"

"He's going to move into my place after the wedding. Joel is kinda traditional like that."

"Mmmhmpf," I reply because I don't know what else to say.

"I can drop you off in town, if you like?" Ruby offers.

"Or you can stay here for the night," my sister suggests.

"You and I can have a brother-sister sleepover but come three tomorrow, your sorry ass needs to be gone because Rubes and I are having a dick-free weekend."

"Really, dick free?"

"Mmmhmpf." My sister nods. "Rubes and I don't often get us time, and we're going to take advantage of it ... but there will be no penises, or is it peeni? What's the plural of penis?"

"How the hell should I know?"

"Because of the three of us, you're the only one with a penis."

"Yes, and I only have one, so knowing the plural isn't high on my need-to-know list of things."

"Well, you suck." She picks up her phone. "Hey, Siri, what's the plural of penis?"

A few seconds later, Siri advises us, "The plural of penis is penises."

"Well, there you go," Ruby says. "but personally, I think peeni sounds better than penises, and on that peen note, I will leave you two to your sleepover. If you need me to get anything tomorrow, just sing out."

"I have it all sorted, Rubes. You just need to bring your gorgeous self and leave all the plans to me."

"Are you scared, Reindeer? Putting your life in Sabbi's hands is dangerous." My sister sticks her tongue out at me like the mature twenty-eight-year-old she is not.

"Nah, I trust her." She walks over to my sister and drapes her arm around her shoulders. "She hasn't led me astray yet so I think I'll be fine ... besides, I know the new sheriff in town, and I'm sure he'd helped me hide a body should the occasion ever arise."

We all laugh and then the two of them hug goodbye. Ruby offers me a shy wave and then she leaves me with my sister.

"Should we rescue your car?" Sabbi asks me

"Nah, it's not going anywhere without a tow, but I might call the station quickly to let them know so they don't send out a deputy to investigate."

"That's gonna go down well."

"Well, I can tell them it's Murray the Mule Deer's fault."

She laughs and leaves me to call the station.

With business sorted, she and I sit by the fire and we finish the bottle of red that was opened while Ruby was here. She also feeds me some of the leftover pasta they had for dinner. You'd swear my sister was Italian with how good of a pasta cook she is.

"Is it just me or does Reindeer seem off?"

"She's just a nervous bride," Sabbi says, but I can tell she doesn't believe it.

"Don't lie to me, Sis. I haven't seen her in years and in the small time she was here, I could tell she's not her usual bubbly self."

"I guarantee you, she's just worried about the wedding, and I think that's because deep down, she knows Joel isn't right for her."

"Why don't you say something to her?"

"Because she thinks she's happy with him, and I don't want to lose her friendship." She pauses and then slaps my thigh. "But maybe *you* can say something to her?"

"And say what? Hey, Reindeer, I know I haven't seen you in years, but I think marrying this guy I have never met is a mistake because you don't glow like you used to glow." And I mean that; the Ruby Olsen I used to know could make the brightest of rooms brighter. The sound of my sister's voice snaps me back to the present.

"Well, yeah, okay. When you put it like that, I guess we just have to smile and be there for her."

"You're a good friend, Sabrina McMahon."

"And you're a good brother, Maddox Whitworth ... but when are you going to settle down and make me an aunty?"

"I think that ship has sailed, Sis."

My mind drifts to the one who got away. I will always regret that moment, but it's something I will have to live with forever. Now that I'm back and *she's* here too, it's going to be hard—pun totally intended—especially since she's about to marry another man.

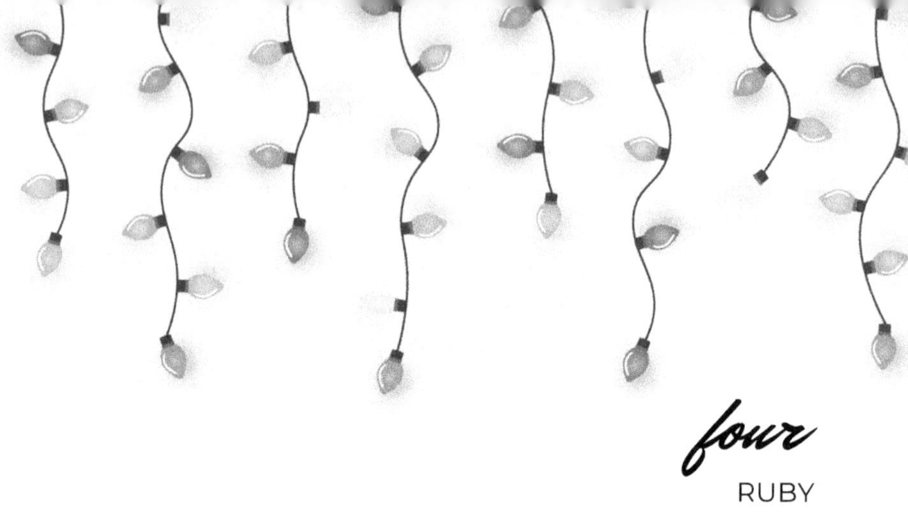

four

RUBY

THE ROADS ARE icy as I drive back to my place, but thankfully, the snow has eased up a little. I'm a good driver, my pop taught me how to drive in some of the most precarious of conditions. Just call me the female version of Marshall Kerr—just without the horrible accident and fractured hip—but I still panic a little when it's like this.

Sticking to the speed limit, I take my time and safely make it back to my cottage. Unlike Mad, I didn't encounter Murray. After his near miss with Mad, he's probably hiding out somewhere cleaning the poop from his ass after his near-death experience with Mad and his truck.

Leaving Sab and Maddox just now, left me with a sense of déjà vu. It reminded me so many times of when we were growing up, and I would head back to my place after having dinner at theirs.

Grabbing my things, I head inside and place my keys in the bowl and my handbag next to it. Next, I shuck off my coat and hang it on the hook near the front door. Kicking off my boots, I slide my feet into my Uggs and let out a contented sigh. A sense

20

of peace washes over me, and I know Nan and Pop are here with me, happy I made it home safely.

Grabbing the gift box from Sab out of my bag, I walk over to my tree, looking for the perfect spot for the ornament. The lights are on an automatic timer and they shimmer and sparkle as I continue to look for *the* spot. Finally, right at eye level, I find where I'm going to place it. Lifting the lid, I carefully pull out the ornament. Holding it up, I gaze at it and smile. My best friend knows me too well, this is stunning and one-hundred-and-ten-percent me.

Placing it on the tree, I smile, even amongst the other decorations, her gift shines brightly and is the focal point on this year's tree. This Christmas is even more perfect now.

Walking into the kitchen, I pour myself a glass of red wine and take a sip. Closing my eyes, I savor the flavor and let the wine infuse my soul and warm me from the inside out. With my glass in hand, I head into the living room and sit down. Grabbing my phone, I shoot off a text to Joel.

RUBY

Hope you had a good day. Just got home from dinner with Sab. Love You.

Picking up the remote, I turn the television on and *Home Alone 2* is playing. It's not Christmas without watching these movies, so I snuggle back and laugh along at Kevin and his antics. My eyes grow heavy, and I drift off to dreamland.

In the middle of the room, I stand in my wedding dress while a man in a suit runs his fingertips sensually up and down my arm. Reaching up, I cup his cheek, and when my palm connects with his skin, the room lights up and my heart races. He leans forward and presses his lips to mine. Fireworks explode around us. The room fades away, and it's just the two of us. His tongue pushes into my mouth. Mine pushes into his and an erotic dance happens in my mouth. His hard length presses into my stomach, and I moan into the kiss.

He slides his hand down my body and slips it under the tule of my dress, his finger runs over my pussy lips and once again, I moan into the kiss. He pushes the soaked material of my panties to the side, and I hold on to his wrist as he thrusts his digit into me.

In and out.

In and out.

With each flick of his wrist, I fall under his spell. Closer and closer to the big "O." Pleasure builds deep within, and when I open my eyes, I stare at a faceless man as I explode.

My eyes snap open and I gasp, as my dream fades away.

Closing my eyes I try and catch my breath. Breathlessly panting, I lie here with my eyes closed, trying to calm my racing heart, but they fly back open when I realize I have my hand in my panties and I'm fingering myself ... just like the faceless man of my dream. I'm on the cusp of an orgasm and need to come. I should feel guilty for getting off over my mystery dream man but I'm too far gone to care.

Lifting my other hand, I squeeze my breast and it's what I need. I writhe on the sofa as an explosive orgasm envelops me, my body shudders as my fingers slide in and out of me. I pinch and squeeze my breast harder as the last of my release fades away.

Collapsing back onto the sofa, that feeling of guilt intensifies and I quickly pull my hand out from between my thighs. I shouldn't be dreaming of faceless men, I should be dreaming of my fiancé doing things like that to me. "I really need to get laid," I mumble to myself.

Sitting up, I swing my legs over the edge of the sofa, and as I move, the ornament Sabrina gave me catches my eye. I think of what the shopkeeper told Sab about it ... and then her questioning if Joel is the one. *Is that why I just dreamed of a faceless man? Is the universe trying to tell me something?* Quickly, I shake off that thought. Joel *is* the one but as I think of my fiancé, I realize over the last few weeks, he's been absent. It kind of feels like he's pulling away from me. I'm hoping it's just nerves due to our upcoming nuptials and the stress of work and the holidays, but is it more? Or am I overreacting?

In seventeen days' time, when I become Mrs. Joel Prior, he and I will be blissfully happy and I can look back on this and laugh. Flipping the television off, I hop up and shuffle into my bedroom. I change into my pajamas and climb into bed, where I once again dream of my faceless man ... but this time, I keep my hands to myself.

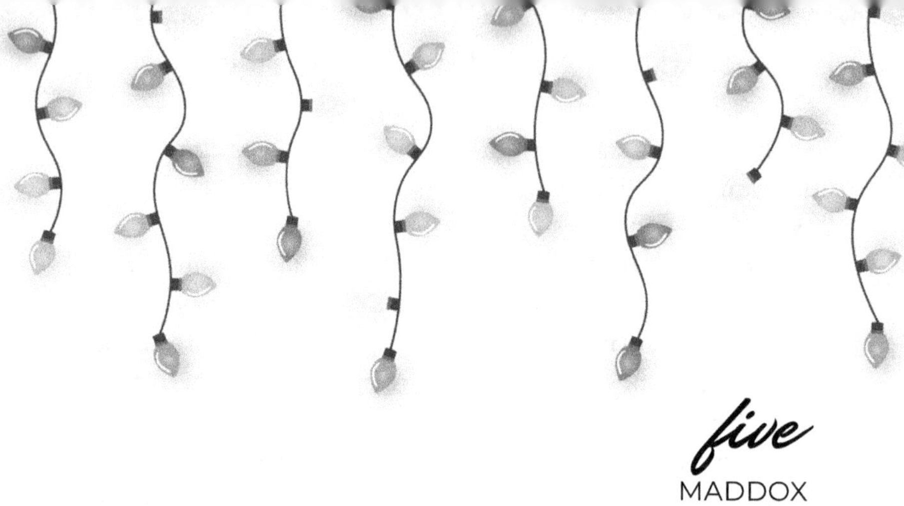

five

MADDOX

BLINKING MY EYES OPEN, I lie here and stare at the ceiling above. My night was restless. I kept dreaming of a woman with killer curves but she was always just out of my reach. Our hands were a hair's breadth apart, but no matter how much each of us wriggled our fingers, we never touched. Every time I thought I was going to catch her, she would once again slip through my grasp.

Touching my head, I wince. It's throbbing and still hurts like a bitch. I can't believe I crashed my car. That's going to go over well when I head into the station later today to meet up with everyone before I officially start next week.

The smell of freshly brewed coffee and pastries has me climbing out of bed and shuffling out to the kitchen.

"Ugh, dude," my sister screeches, covering her eyes. "Put some clothes on."

Looking down, I smirk when I realize I'm only in my briefs and my morning wood is standing to attention, waving hello. "Oops, sorry, Sis, I'm used to living alone and not having to worry about..." I point to my junk, earning myself a disgusted shudder from my sister.

"Go put some clothes on, you freak. A girl does not need to see her brother like that first thing in the morning ... or ever. I need to bleach my eyes."

"Under the sink," I unhelpfully sing out as I walk back into my room to pull on a pair of gray sweatpants. Walking back out to the kitchen, I smile at my sister. "Better?"

"Not really ... you've just ruined gray sweatpants for me." Staring at her I wait for an explanation, because right now, I'm confused as hell. Then, it clicks in my brain just as she says, "Heroes in romance novels always wear gray sweatpants 'cause hello, they are hot, but now I will associate them with you and you're my brother."

"Are you saying I'm hot?"

"You know you are. So many of my friends at school had a crush on you back in the day."

But I only ever wanted one friend of yours, I think to myself as I shuffle over to the coffeepot and pour myself a mug. "Top up?"

"Please." She nods and slides her mug over to me.

"Thanks again for letting me crash here last night."

"Well, I couldn't leave you stranded in the snow." She chuckles. "Still can't believe you crashed after a run-in with Murray."

"Murray is dead next time I see him."

"Leave the poor deer alone, besides, if you do anything to him, you will have two very sad nieces."

"You know I would never harm an animal, and now I know Cass and Mon are fans of his, I will not touch a hair on his stupid head."

"Good," she states with a nod.

"Think you can give me a lift into town?"

"Sure, I need to stop at Hanson's to stock up for girls' weekend so once we get here, we don't need to go anywhere."

"Can I ask you a question?"

"You can, but whether I answer or not is another thing."

"I swear, your sass has increased tenfold over the years."

"You're welcome." She takes a bow and jumps up onto the counter next to where I'm leaning. "What's your question?"

"What do you really think of Ruby's fiancé?"

"Why do you ask?"

"Humor me," I tell her.

She purses her lips and furrows her brows. "Okay, fine, I'll tell you what I feel, but if you utter a word of this to anyone, itchy powder in your undies will seem like a walk in the park with what I will do to you."

"Scout's honor." I hold my fingers up.

"Joel's a dick, if you ask me. I've never really liked him, but Ruby is head over heels, ass over tit, in love with him." She pauses. "It's funny, when I think back to then, we got back from Christmas break in our first year at college, Ruby was different but a few months later, she met Joel and the old Rubes came back. But over the years, before my eyes, I've seen her slowly dying again." She takes a deep breath. "And while I'm being brutally honest, he's not who I pictured Rubes ending up with. He's so, square and straitlaced and Ruby is not a square bear. She's adventurous and free-spirited and wild."—*Ohh, I know she's wild*—"She needs someone who is going to challenge her and support her."

"He doesn't support her?"

"He does, but he also thinks her store is silly. 'Romance isn't a way to make a living' he always tells her."

"Does he not know romance is one of the highest-selling genres out there?"

"Are we a closeted romance reader?"

"I'm a reader, Sab. As long as the story hooks me, I'll read it … and if it has a side of porn, I'm down with that too."

"Romance does not equal porn, Mad."

"Fine, how's this then, as long as the story hooks me, I'll read it … and if it has a side of spice, I'm down with that."

"Better, but seriously, you read smut?"

With a shrug and a cheeky wink, I swallow the last of my coffee. Placing my mug in the dishwasher, I turn to my sister. "What time did you want to head into town?"

"Give me ten to shower and we can go."

"Great, see you in an hour," I tease.

"Sooo funny," she throws back at me, but we both know I'm right. My sister takes forever to get ready … and I was right. Forty minutes later, we climb into her Range Rover and we head into town. She drops me off at the station and we go our separate ways, with her agreeing to help me unpack a few things later today.

Walking into the station, a feeling of being home washes over me. When I walk up to the front counter, Deputy Dennis Mitchell and Stan Wolensky start a slow clap, and then Stan mimics a crash with his hands—and what I think is meant to be a crashing sound—but it sounds more like a deer giving birth.

"Crashing into town like a champ, I see," Dennis teases, offering me his hand for a shake.

"Hardy har har, Dennis. I see news travels fast around here."

"Umm, hello, it's Evergreen Lake. Nothing is ever a secret around here."

That's the only downfall to moving back here, news here travels faster than the speed of light and like Telephone, often the story changes and morphs into a wicked tale. "Who spilled the beans?" I ask, as I walk around the desk into the back, shaking Stan's hand as I pass him.

"Three guesses?" Dennis says, holding up three fingers.

Taking a guess, I say the first busybody's name to come to mind. "Sheila?"

"Ding-Ding-Ding, we have a winner."

"How did she find out?"

"Delivery Dan saw your car when he was out and about this morning. He mentioned to Mary seeing the car when he did the delivery at Sips earlier and the gossip queens were there, and well, now everyone knows. Welcome back, Sheriff."

"What are the chances this will be kept quiet?" Dennis and Stan both crack up laughing. "Fuck," I hiss and squeeze the back of my neck to ease the tension knot forming. I slept like shit last night and my body is a little sore after my crash.

"On that note," Dennis says once he's stopped laughing at me. "Your car has been towed to Chris's and he's already working on it for you."

"Thanks, Dennis, appreciate it. Is Sheriff Roberts in?"

Dennis shakes his head, "Nah, he's in town making the final arrangements for tonight."

"Okay, thanks, I'll catch up with him there."

"Looking forward to working with you, Maddox," Dennis says.

"Me too," Stan adds.

"I'm looking forward to it too. I'll catch up with you both tonight."

Saying our goodbyes, I head into town to meet up with Sheriff Roberts, but I get sidetracked when I come across a quaint little bookstore on Main Street.

six

RUBY

BRINGING the book to my nose, I close my eyes and breathe in deeply. The scent of a new paperback within *my* bookstore is the best smell in the world, along with freshly cut grass, pine trees—especially at Christmas time—and a freshly poured glass of red wine. I draw the line at gasoline, wet dog, and cigarette smoke—eww.

"Did you just sniff that book?" A deep voice startles me, and I squeal like a banshee. The novel I was holding goes flying and lands with a thud on the hardwood floor beside the front counter.

With my hand resting against my chest, I try to calm the rapid beating of my heart. Looking up, I smile when I see Maddox standing in the doorway of Read Between the Wines.

"Shit, Maddox. You scared me."

"Sorry, but answer the question, did you just smell that book?" He walks over to the counter and leans against it. The material of his shirt pulls tight across his biceps and chest when he crosses his arms. My gaze lingers on his arms and when I realize, I'm still ogling him, I lift my gaze to his face and notice him staring intently at me.

"Yeah, I did," I nonchalantly reply with a shrug.

"You do that often?"

"Yeah, I do," I freely admit without any shame. To a book lover, the smell of a book, old or new, is euphoric. It hits how I imagine a coke addict feels when the drug hits their system.

"That's creepy and weird."

"Is not," I throw back at him.

Maddox bends down and picks the book up. He hands it to me across the counter and our fingers brush, an electrical current zaps from him to me. Judging by the look on his face, he felt it too.

Taking the book from him, I inspect it for any damage. Running the pad of my finger over the spine and then the other edges, I smile when I thankfully realize there are no marks.

"Are you now *fondling* the book?" He places emphasis on the word fondle, and it comes out in a sexual way.

"No, I was checking it for damage." Placing it down on the counter, I stare over at Maddox and my heart skips a beat. He really is gorgeous and has aged well. Like a fine bottle of red. His hair is still the same style but the color seems darker and softer. His eyes are still mesmerizing, the flecks of gold in his chocolate-brown orbs are fleckier than usual today, and his lips are still that kissable shade of dusty red.

"No, you were molesting that poor book."

"I think you hit your head harder than we thought last night because you're talking shit right now."

"Says the one smelling and fondling a book."

"Let's agree to disagree as to what I was doing with the book."

"Fine, I will leave you and your book fetish alone."

"How's the head today?" Reaching out, I run my finger over the Band-Aid on his forehead. Our gazes connect and it's as if time stands still. I'm transported back to when I was nineteen and we had sex for the first time. The night *all* my dreams came true.

"Like I told you both last night, it doesn't hurt."

"Hurt and injured are two different things, Mad."

"Pretty sure they are one and the same but I promise, I'm all good. Ready to get moved in and unpacked as soon as the movers arrive."

"If I didn't have to work, I'd help."

"You don't need to do that but I appreciate the offer."

He pushes off the counter and walks farther into the store. Following him, I stand next to him as he looks around. He shoves his hands into the pockets of his jeans, and I watch him as he takes in my store. Read Between the Wines is my baby, and I'm proud of what I've turned it into.

When I first got this space it was an empty shell and now it's my happy place. It's filled with millions upon millions of words. Stories across all the genres but I mostly specialize in romance novels—my favorite. We have books of all heat levels, we do not discriminate here. And if someone wants something I don't stock, I will source it and order it in for them. Reading is reading and I will not begrudge anyone for what they like, but I do draw the line at dino porn. That shit is just weird and creepy.

In the adjoining room is the wine bar and seating area. The full length of one side is the bar, serving a variety of wines from all over the world. We also have a small selection of craft beers and non-alcoholic options as well. Coffee can be brought in from Sips and food from Lips and Hips or Granny Taught Us How, located inside Hanson's Mercantile. There are a few high-top and café-style tables in front of the bar, and off from there is a den with a fireplace and several comfy throne-like chairs. On quiet days, I like curling up by the fireplace with my current read and losing myself within the pages of my book.

Once a month, I host a wine and book night that we affectionally call the Wi-ook Club. It started out with only three people, but now there's up to thirty people and over the holidays, the place is packed. Each person brings a plate and for hours upon hours we talk books, wine, and all things fine.

The bookshelves are all made by a local craftsman, using timber from trees in the surrounding area. The floors are polished hardwood and are a bitch to keep shiny. But thankfully I have Robbie, he's my robot vacuum/mopper thing—affectionately called Robbie the Robo Vac—and he's the best present Joel has ever bought me.

"Ruby," a deep voice says and I startle, again, and when I jump, I lose my balance, but before I end up on my ass, Maddox reaches out and saves me.

"Joel," I breathlessly pant as Maddox puts me back upright on my feet. "What are you doing here?"

"Came to take you to an early lunch?" It comes out like a question but I smile at the sentiment as I walk over and kiss him hello.

"That's so sweet of you, but Charlene called in sick so I can't get away today."

"Ohh," he dejectedly scoffs in annoyance. His gaze flicks between Maddox and me. "Who are you?" he rudely asks.

"Sheriff Maddox Whitworth." He offers his hand to Joel.

"You're Sabrina's brother, right?"

"That's me."

"What are you doing here?" Again, he's coming across rude but Maddox doesn't seem to notice.

"Not that it's any of your business, but I came to thank Reindeer here for her services last night." Joel's eyes widen at that.

"Mad had a car accident on his way into town last night. He ended up at Sab's rental cottage and we patched him up."

"What happened?"

"A deer ran out in front of me, and I ended up in a snowbank."

"Thought law enforcement could drive in the snow?"

"I'd like to see you stay on the road when a deer suddenly steps out in front of you."

An awkward silence surrounds us. My gaze flits between the two men before my eyes connect with Mad's. "Thanks again for last night. I'll see you around, Reindeer."

"You are most welcome, Sheriff," I tell him. Stepping to him, I pull him in for a hug. "It's good to have you back."

"It's good to be back." He pulls away and looks to Joel. "Joel," he tersely says in lieu of a goodbye, and without another word, he walks out.

"Well, that was rude," Joel states when the door clicks shut behind Maddox.

"Yes, it was," I say, looking at Joel.

"Why you looking at me like that?"

"*You* were the rude one, Joel."

"Me?" he hisses. "What did I do?"

"You were snippy and snarky with him when he's done nothing wrong."

"I don't like the way he was looking at you, and why is he calling you Reindeer? I thought only your pop did that."

"Maddox has always called me that too, except he went a step further and used to sing Ruby the Red-nosed Reindeer." I laugh when I think back on that. "It used to piss me off but at the same time, I secretly loved it."

"That is kinda cute," Joel agrees, giving me that smile of his I first fell in love with. My moment of contentment dissipates when he tacks on, "He likes you, Rubes."

"I like him too," I say. *More than I should, considering I'm getting married soon.* "As a friend," I quickly tack on, "and hopefully now he's back, Sab will visit more often.

"Let's hope not," Joel hisses, his face scrunched up, letting me know exactly how he feels about the new sheriff in town. "Well, since you can't get away, I'll see you later."

He turns to walk away without kissing or hugging me good-bye, but I quickly sing out, "Orrrrr, you could get soup and grilled cheese sandwiches from Lips and Hips, bring them back here, and we can sit by the fire and have a romantic lunch date for two."

"You really want to do that?"

"I'd love to." Walking over to him, I drape my arms over his shoulders and stare into his eyes. He slides his around my waist, but the usual feeling of being home and loved when I'm in his arms is missing. "Feels like I haven't seen you in forever."

"You saw me two nights ago when we met at the lodge to finalize things for the wedding."

"We did, yes, but we haven't had any *us* time lately." I place emphasis on the *us* part but it seems to go straight over his head. "If I were insecure about us, I'd think you were cheating on me." I chuckle at the thought of Joel cheating on me but when he quickly refutes that thought, I begin to wonder. As quick as that thought appears, I quickly quash it. Joel is *not* that kind of person, at all.

"I'd never do that," he quickly replies. With a kiss to the tip of my nose, he begins to walk backward to the door. "Back in ten with lunch."

He saunters out of the store, and I watch his retreating form. Joel and I are getting married in sixteen days, but suddenly, I don't know if marrying him is the right thing to do. I know I love him, but am I *in* love with him? Right now should be the happiest time of my life, but here I am questioning everything.

Walking into the wine bar, I sit in my favorite chair and stare into the flames of the fire, hoping they'll give me the answers I desire but before they can answer me, my fiancé returns with our lunch. He unpacks the food while I jump up and pour us each a glass of red.

Walking over to the high-top table, I take my seat across from Joel. Before me is a decadent-looking grilled cheese sandwich and a bowl of soup—mushroom soup—eew. Nothing against Norah and her soups but mushroom anything is disgusting; those fungi lil' fuckers can go back into the dark where they come from. Everyone knows it's *not* the soup I would have ordered and, of all people, my fiancé should know this. It's funny because he loves them and I despise them. I remember when we first started dating, he asked me over to his place for dinner one night. He was so happy and was raving about this new pasta dish and when he served it, my face fell. It was a mushroom pasta dish that was full of all these exotic mushrooms. I later found out some of them weren't cheap. He was so proud so I reluctantly nibbled my way through, but he was finished and I still has heaps left on my plate. I finally told him I hate mushrooms with a passion and he felt so bad. We laugh about it now but at the time, I was questioning if I could be with him ... but he made up for it by ordering me pizza. He gained bonus points when he ordered pepperoni with black olives, my all-time favorite pizza. Especially because he has an aversion to olives like I do mushrooms.

Eating my sandwich and sipping on my wine, I stare at my soup, building up the courage to try it, but I just can't do it. Not only does it look like dirty dishwater but it smells like it too. The thing that hurts the most is Joel hasn't noticed my unease or aversion to the soup. He never said a thing about my not eating it and then without saying a word, he reaches over, grabs my untouched bowl, and begins to eat it too.

When he's finished, he packs up the containers, still not mentioning my uneaten soup. Then, with a lackluster peck on my cheek, he leaves, wishing me a good weekend with Sab. I was hoping he'd join us for dinner at the tree lighting tonight but I never got a chance to ask him ... I was too busy focusing on the gross soup.

Dropping back into the chair, I shake my head and sigh in frustration. Sitting here, I think over our lunch just now. Not only did he get a soup I despise but we didn't really talk at all. We ate in silence, something that has been happening more and more lately. Leaning back into my chair, I think of the book I just read and the lead-up to their wedding. The hero and heroine were both so excited, but I don't think I can say that for either Joel or me. And as the owner of a bookstore that specializes in romance novels, my life right now should be filled with joy and an abundance of romance. Yes, Joel has a lot to live up to, but right now, he's failing ... and so am I when it comes to romance.

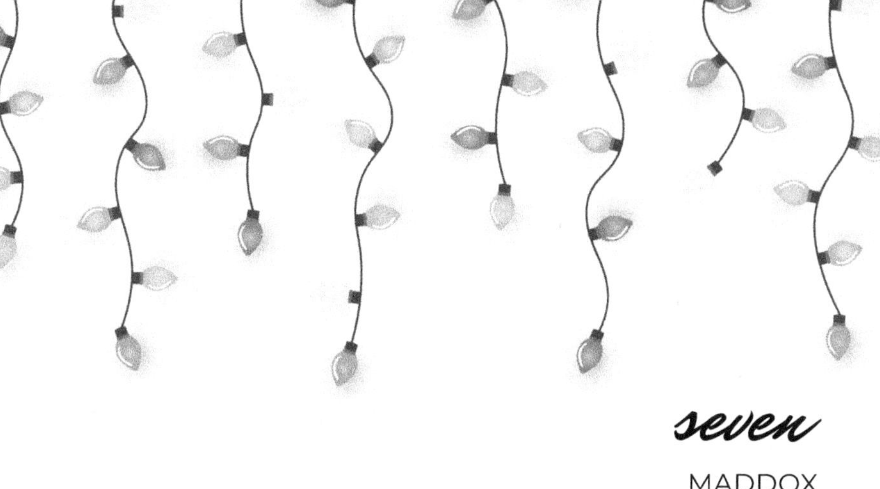

seven

MADDOX

THE LAST PIECE of furniture has been carried into my new apartment and after saying goodbye to the movers, I fall down onto said last piece of furniture—my sofa. It's a heavy setting but it's worth it. This thing is like sitting in a fluffy cloud that hugs you and I love it, especially after a long night shift. I usually sleep on it rather than in my bed.

I've only been back for less than twenty-four hours and already it feels like home, but something is missing. I can't put my finger on what that is, but I do know I'm where I'm meant to be. That same feeling slammed into me when I walked into the station earlier, and the same thing happened when I opened the front door here. It felt right, and I knew I chose the perfect place to live. This is where I'm meant to be and really, it's not surprising since I grew up here. The only reason I left was to go to the police academy. If I'd have gotten a job in Evergreen Lake as soon as I graduated, I would have been back in a heartbeat. Evergreen Lake is home, always has been and it always will be. Not much has changed over the years, Evergreen Lake is just as majestic as I remember, and this time of year is always magical.

Maybe I feel off because I don't have any decorations up yet.

Normally, as soon as Thanksgiving is over I start decorating, but with moving this year, I don't have one decoration up. But to be honest, the thought of decorating while unpacking is about as appealing as a prostate check.

"Avon calling," a voice calls out, and when I look up, I see my smiling sister standing in the doorway of my new place with a mini potted Christmas tree.

"That wasn't funny when you visited me at the academy or in Reno, and it's still not funny now."

"Please, it's hilarious … especially since we all know you love using Avon anti-wrinkle crap."

"Not a wrinkle on my face, Sis, maybe you should try it? You know, for those crow's-feet appearing around your eyes."

"I don't have any wrinkles," she huffs.

Plopping my Christmas tree down by the front door, she heads straight for my bathroom. From my vantage point in the living room, I see her looking in the mirror; she's checking for the nonexistent wrinkles. Walking back into the living area, she glares at me as she pulls off her coat, draping it over one of my barstools. "So, where do we begin?"

Looking around, I shrug. "I have no idea."

"How about we start with your bedroom? Get that ready so you will at least have somewhere to crash tonight."

"Good plan."

She grabs her phone and looks around for my sound system, but I haven't set it up yet. She rolls her eyes and I shake my head. Jumping up, I grab my portable speaker from the box that has all the essentials needed when moving and pop it on the coffee table.

With a smile, she scrolls through her phone and then hits play. "Christmas Lights" by Coldplay filters out through the speaker. She's clearly in a Christmas mood and with Chris singing away, we move down the hallway and start putting my bedroom together.

The movers were great and actually put my bed together so all Sab and I have to do is find the bedding, and then figure out how and where to set it up. Prior to her having kids, she worked as an interior designer so I stand back and let her work her magic. And by stand back I mean, I follow her directions—demands—and move things around and about until she's happy.

Once my bedroom is sorted, she moves into the main living area, and within an hour, she has my living room and dining area staged, whatever that means. Now all I have to do is unpack my shit, and no doubt I will move things five times before I'm happy.

"Red wine?" I ask her when I finish unpacking a box of glassware.

She shakes her head. "Thanks, but I need to head out. I still need to grab a few things for the weekend before I pick Rubes up. You wanna come to the tree lighting with us tonight?"

"I thought it was girls' weekend?"

"It is but Friday is technically still part of the workweek so there's your loophole to attend with us." She pauses. "That's if you don't have any other plans." She waggles her eyebrows at me.

"You look like you're having a stroke," I tell her.

She flips me the bird. "Whatever. You joining us or not?"

"Yeah, I might join you, sounds like fun."

The annual tree lighting ceremony is always a good night in town. Actually, every event in the month of December is great here. For a small town, they sure know how to celebrate and party. From the tree lighting to kick off the Christmas festival to gingerbread stands each weekend, and who can forget the infamous Evergreen Lake key party. I've never attended one but I've heard stories and let's just say, I prefer my spice in a book ... and at home. I'm no prude, but yeah, that's not my jam.

After locking in a time for later, Sabbi heads out and leaves me to unpack a few more things. We moved her housewarming tree next to the fireplace, and since it's tiny compared to the usual Douglas fir I would have, I decide to just decorate it with ornaments. Then I string some colored Christmas lights around the fireplace and when I switch them on, it suddenly feels Christmassy, and the void I felt before is no longer here.

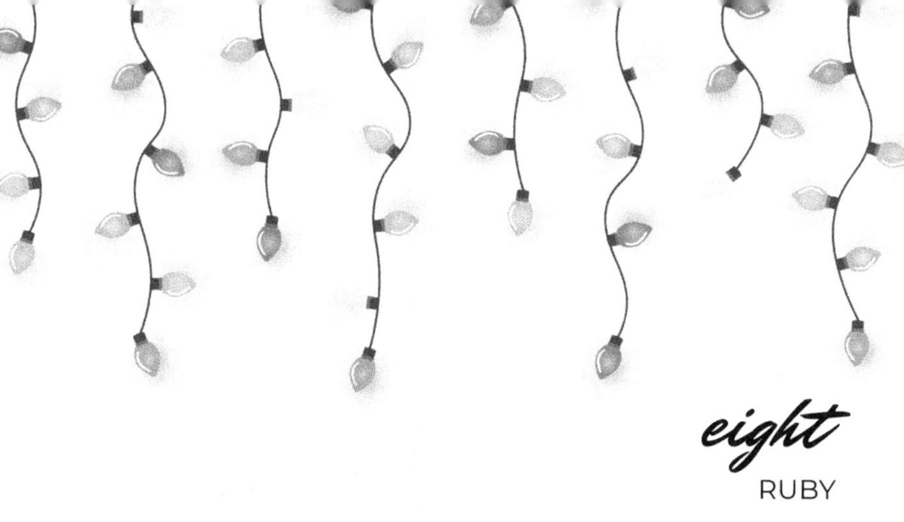

eight

RUBY

A FEW HOURS LATER, Sab and I are sitting where I fell earlier. She found me sitting here when she popped in early and as soon as she saw me, she walked behind the bar, grabbed a bottle of wine and two glasses. She poured us each a glass of wine and sipping on my wine with my bestie, my mood started to improve. Especially when I handed her the latest Cassie Laelyn novel from her Fallen Guardians series. Sab excitedly gushes over all her heroes and then she gets onto Blaine, the bad guy. Cassie somehow has made the bad guy hot and intriguing and I cannot wait for his book. I'm totally rooting for him and fate to end up together and if that doesn't happen, I'm gonna be pissed off but whichever route she takes, I know it's gonna be phenomenal.

By the fire, she pours me another glass and I tell her about my encounter with Maddox and then I broach lunch with Joel. "Joel and I had a lunch date earlier but he, umm, got me mushroom soup to go with my grilled cheese."

"He got you what?" Sab screeches, her tone reaching banshee level, indicating she's just as shocked as I was.

"Fungi soup," I repeat.

"But you hate mushrooms. Everyone in a hundred-mile radius knows that."

"Mmmhmpf," I nonchalantly reply.

"Does he not know you at all?" A shrug is all I can manage in reply, and my ever observant best friend knows something is up. "Spit it out, Olsen."

"Spit what out?" I'm trying to play dumb because I'm not sure I want to voice it, but she gives me her "don't insult me" look, and then my mouth opens and I spew out all of my fears. "Am I making the right decision marrying Joel? Because right now, I'm so confused. I don't know what's up and what's down. I know I love him but is love enough? Nanna and Pop loved one another and even without words you could tell that. Can you tell that with Joel and me? I want an all-encompassing love like they had, and I don't know if I have that, and if I'm marrying the man, shouldn't I know what type of love we have?"

When I finish my word vomiting, Sab just sits here, blankly looking at me. Then, without a word, she jumps up and walks into the other room. I hear the flip of the lock and the sounds of the "Open" sign being turned off. Then she walks back into the room and behind the bar, where she grabs another bottle of wine. She returns, fills my glass to the top, and does the same to hers. Then she sits back down and stares at me.

"Why do I feel like I'm in trouble?"

"You're not in trouble with me but I do think you're *in* trouble. Rubes, you just dropped a massive-ass bomb on me, and I need time to process so I can best help you." She takes a sip of her drink. "When did these doubts start?"

"I don't know exactly, but last night, I dreamed about a faceless man who evoked feelings in me that I haven't felt in a very long time, and when Joel kissed me earlier when he arrived, I felt nothing. Not even a tingle and then the soup thing happened, and now I'm doubting everything."

"Do you love him?" I nod because I do love him. She shakes her head. "No, I mean do you love-love him? Or are you in love with the idea of him as your husband?"

My glass is halfway to my mouth, and I pause as I process her words. "I … I love him." Then I quietly tack on, "I think." My eyes well with tears, and I look over at my best friend.

"Ohhh, Rubes." She stands up and walks over to me. Dropping to her knees before me, she takes my wine from my hands and places it on the table next to hers. "Talk to me, why have you not said anything?"

All I can do is shrug because I don't know. I don't think I even realized Joel and I had fallen into a funk until today. "You know I've always been able to confide in you about everything" —*well, almost everything*—"but I honestly didn't really think about it until just now. I've been stewing on it ever since, and I guess I didn't want to voice it out loud because if I did, then it would be real, but we're getting married soon—"

"Do you *want* to marry Joel?"

My head begins to bob up and down, but then I stop and shrug. "I don't know," I whisper. "These last few months, it feels like he's pulling away. I put it down to the stress of the wedding because I'm stressed too, but last night…" Shit, I have to stop myself because I can't tell her seeing Maddox again after all these years brought up all the memories of us from all those years ago. This is why secrets are bad.

"Last night what?"

Looking at her, I decide to go with a half-truth. "You gave me that ornament and then Maddox knocked—"

"You want my brother?"

Yes. "No, what I mean is, I made that wish and then not Joel appeared. If that thing is magical, shouldn't my one true love have appeared?"

"We both know magic isn't real."

"Magical love is all around us." I wave my hand around my store.

"Books and real life never really match up, and as much as I would love to have you as my sister-in-law, you can do so much better than my brother. He's"—she pauses and shudders—"my brother, but since we're being honest, I don't think Joel is the one for you either." She titters. "It's funny, when I got you that ornament, I didn't expect anything to come of it, and I know I just said magic isn't real, but maybe it's subconsciously telling you Joel isn't the one and your Mr. Forever is still out there."

"Sab, I'm supposed to get married in sixteen days. Sixteen days. Everything is booked. My dress is hanging in my closet. The cater—"

"Plans change," she says, as if it's that easy. She takes my hand in hers and squeezes. "Just think about what you really want. If it's Joel, I will be there in sixteen days' time at your side smiling brightly in my non-shitty bridesmaid dress, and if it's not him, I will be in the driver's seat ready to whisk you away."

"You really are the best friend a girl could ask for."

"You still think that after my gift has opened up a can of worms?"

"I think I would have felt like this regardless of your gift, but I'm happy to place blame on you to alleviate my stress."

"And as your bestie, I'm happy to take said blame. Now, let's get out of here, we have a girls' weekend to start, but do me a favor?" I nod. "Try not think about it this weekend. Have fun. Focus on you and then next week, focus on the bigger picture."

"I'll try," I tell her. "Now, let's do this."

Together we clean up, making sure everything is tidy for Charlene tomorrow. I'm so thankful she's here. If I had to deal with these thoughts by myself, I'd stress myself to death, but with my best friend by my side, I know I'll be fine.

nine

MADDOX

MY SISTER HONKS from outside and I shake my head. A normal person would just text to say they've arrived or even climb out of their car and knock on the door, but no, Sabrina McMahon does both—she's texts AND honks. Fifteen minutes ago she messaged me to say she and Reindeer are on their way, and by my calculations, the trip should have taken twenty-two minutes, so it seems my sister's lead foot was in force tonight.

Grabbing my bomber jacket, I slip it on over my dark Henley and zip it up. Locking the door behind me, I shove my hands into my pockets and head out to meet my sister. The front passenger door opens and Reindeer hops out. My step almost falters as I take her in because, fuck me sideways, she's stunning. She's wearing black leather pants that look like a second skin and a black bomber jacket over what I think is a red sweater. Her locks have been straightened, and the ends brush her shoulders. It's clipped back on one side. "Is that a poinsettia in your hair?"

"Mmmhmpf." She nods with a smile. "Only time of year I can wear it. I always bring it out tonight 'cause it goes with my sweater." She unzips her jacket, and I smile when I see it's a

45

Christmas sweater. Where most people have ugly ones, Reindeer's is gorgeous. Hers is red and white and it has a combination of reindeer, snowflakes, and love hearts on it. It's quintessentially her and I find myself smiling, and not just because the neckline showcases her stunning tits.

"You look beautiful," I tell her as she goes to open the back door. "What are you doing?"

"Your legs are longer than mine." My gaze drops to her legs, and I notice her boots. They're black, have a wedge heel, and come up over her knees. Suddenly, I'm picturing her in nothing but her boots. Her perky tits begging for me to suck them, but at the sound of the car horn honking, I quickly shake off the dirty thoughts. Internally slapping myself up the side of the head as I remind myself she's getting married in a few short weeks. It pains me I missed my chance with her, but thankfully, I have my memories of our time together.

"Well, thank you. Let me." Opening the door for her, I watch her ass as she climbs in, and once she's seated, I close the door behind her. Readjusting my dick, I climb in, and when I turn toward my sister, she has a look on her face that I can't read.

"Maddox," she says by way of greeting.

"Sabrina," I say her name with a nod. "I was expecting you in another five minutes."

"What can I say, traffic was on my side."

"Or your foot was flat to the floor."

"Or that," she replies with a shrug. "Ready to get our Christmas fair on?"

She fiddles with her phone and "Winter Wonderland" begins to play through the speakers. Soon, the three of us are singing along as my sister, aka Lightning McQueen, drives us to the festival.

Parking her car, we all climb out. Sabrina links her arm with Rubes and me and the three of us walk toward the festival.

The tree has been lit and this year, I reckon, it would rival the one in Rockefeller Center in New York ... just on a smaller scale, but it is no less stunning. Holly, the manager at the Chamber of Commerce, along with Amos from Winter Farms outdid themselves this year. Amos deserves an extra pat on the back; he donated the trees for the street decorations too.

"You having fun, Reindeer?" I ask, bumping her shoulder as we watch Sabrina dance with Delivery Dan. We're standing next to the makeshift dance floor with a cup of mulled wine in our hands. To our right, the G-team—the Gossip team—as I affectionately call Mildred, Berniece, and Sheila. The three of them are dancing together and giggling like schoolgirls. When I get to their age, I hope I have just as much life and spirit in me as they do.

"Mmmhmpf," she replies, but it doesn't seem sincere. Then she smiles but it's not her usual vibrant one.

"Wanna try that again?"

"No, I am. It's been a great night, I just wish Joel was here."

"Where is he tonight?" She shrugs and a silence falls between us as the song changes to "Driving Home For Christmas" by Chris Rea. "Would a spin around the dance floor cheer you up?"

Again, she shrugs, but not giving her a chance to say no, I take her almost empty cup and place them both in the trash, then I grab her hand and pull her onto the dance floor. Spinning her out, I pull her back in, and slide my hand around her waist and rest it on her hip, not giving her a chance to pull away from me. I hold one of her hands between us and she drapes her other arm over my shoulder. She rests her head on my chest and we sway to the music. Several songs pass us by and after twirling and whirling around the dance floor, we find ourselves near the entrance to the dance area when Sheila yells out at the top of her lungs, "Kiss!" Her voice carries over the sound of the music and the music stops when she once again shouts, "Kiss!"

Everyone pauses what they're doing and they look toward Sheila. She's smiling like a carnival clown and then she points at me and Reindeer. Furrowing my brows, I look inquisitively over at her. She moves her finger upward and when I lift my gaze, my eyes widen when I see what's above our heads. Reindeer and I are standing under the mistletoe hanging in the entranceway.

The silence that fell over the festival is broken when someone begins to chant, "Kiss. Kiss. Kiss." Soon after, *everyone* is chanting, "Kiss. Kiss. Kiss."

My sister calls out, "Pucker up," and then she makes kissy sounds.

Looking down at Reindeer, I see her cheeks are pink with embarrassment but for the first time tonight, she's smiling.

"Guess we better keep up with tradition."

"Guess so," she replies. She lifts her gaze to mine and as we stare at one another, everyone around us fades into the distance and I'm taken back to a time in our past...

...Everyone has gone to bed and I've been tasked with making sure Reindeer gets home safely. The two of us are standing just below the back deck. We're gazing into each other's eyes under the moonlit night sky. My heart skips a beat as I lose myself in her eyes. I know this is wrong, she's my sister's best friend, but she's grown into a sexy as hell woman and it's been hard—pun intended—to keep my hands off of her ever since I got home.

"Maddox," she breathlessly utters my name. She rests her hand on my chest and takes a step closer to me.

Lifting my hand, I cup her cheek in my palm and an electrical current zaps from her to me. Like two magnets, our heads begin to move and I have no control. Her eyes close just as I press my lips to hers. As soon as our lips touch, every nerve ending in my body comes alive. Her tongue seeks access to my mouth, and I willingly open. She slides her hand into my hair at my nape and gently tugs on the strands.

Our tongues battle it out, slipping into each other's mouth with ease. Her body presses into mine but the moment is broken when Sabrina calls out her name...

"Ruby." The sound of my sister's voice snaps me back to the present and just like all those years ago, the two of us guiltily jump apart, but unlike last time, we didn't kiss. "Just kiss him on the cheek and then you can bleach your mouth with alcohol."

Quickly, I lean forward and beat her to it. I press my lips to her cheek, and like always, my lips tingle when my skin touches hers, and an electrical current zaps from her to me.

Her eyes widen at the spark that jolts between us. She covers her cheek and lifts her gaze to mine. I'm about to lift my hand and cup her cheek when she whispers my name, "Maddox..." That one word is full of everything but before I can utter a word, she turns around and races away from me.

ten

RUBY

TEARS FILL my eyes as I race away from Maddox. We didn't do anything wrong but I wanted him to kiss me. I wanted him to kiss me like we used to—in secret. I haven't thought of Maddox Whitworth like this in years, not since before Joel and I got together, but since he came back into town yesterday, he's all I can think about.

Turning down a side street, I lean against the brick building. My heart is racing and my hands are clammy. Tilting my head back, I stare up at the night sky. The twinkling stars are laughing down at me for being a fool. I'm marrying another man in a couple of weeks but here I am, upset my first love didn't kiss me properly under the mistletoe. "I'm certifiably crazy," I mumble to myself.

Banging my head against the brick wall, I berate myself for being stupid and upset.

With my heart rate under control, I know it's time to get back but it's flipping cold where I'm hiding.

Pushing off the wall, I take a deep breath and exhale. Nodding to myself, I exit my hiding spot and decide to head back to the fair.

Stepping around the corner, I slam into a muscular chest with a thud and without looking up, I know who it is. Maddox's scent invades my nose and that guilt from before slams into me once again. "Maddox," I breathlessly whisper.

"You okay, Reindeer?"

"Yeah, I'm fine. I—"

"I'm sorry if I made you uncomfortable."

Shaking my head, I rest my hand on his forearm. "It's not you, it's me. I got caught up in the moment, and now I feel guilty."

"Why do you feel guilty?"

"Because we nearly kissed and I'm engaged."

"We—" But before he can finish his sentence, Sab finds us.

"There you two are. Where did you race off to?"

"Nowhere," I tell her but from the skeptical look on her face, she doesn't believe me. Hell, I don't even believe me. Ever since Maddox returned, my world has been turned upside down. It was already chaotic and now, it's Grand Central Station chaotic.

"You ready to head home? I'm kinda beat."

"Sure," I reply, "but please tell me we can drink wine until we fall into a coma when we get there?"

"As long as we can pair it with dark chocolate, popcorn, and pajamas."

"Deal."

Without another word, we head toward Sab's car and after dropping Maddox off, we head back to her rented cottage. As soon as we step inside, we change into our jammies and we proceed to drink copious amounts of red wine. We demolish a bar of dark chocolate—each—and half a bag of salty popcorn.

It does little to ease my guilt but it does cause me to fall into a deep sleep, where I once again dream of my faceless man. Unlike last time, I don't wake with my fingers in my panties but said panties are damp with arousal and my heart is racing. "Who are you?" I mumble to myself.

Climbing out of bed, I slip my feet into my slippers, pull on my robe, and shuffle into the kitchen for a glass of water. Guzzling the cool liquid down, I walk over to the bay window and stare out at the early morning sky. Dropping to my butt, I plop down onto the window seat and pull my legs up. Hugging my legs, I gaze out at the water. The sun is just peeking over the horizon, and the sky is beginning to lighten. I wish my mind would lighten. I can't turn my brain off, and my thoughts flick from one item to another and back again.

I'm exhausted from the constant thinking.

Not even my book is calming my mind; that's how worked up I am. Usually, I can lose myself in my book, but as soon as I get to a romantic part, my mind drifts off. If I'm not imagining my faceless man, it's Maddox or Joel. Hell, I think I even thought about my own harem of men and as much as that was hot, I was slammed with guilt. I should be dreaming of a life with my fiancé, not getting railed by three hot men at one time —even if my fiancé was one of the men railing me. It's wrong, plain and simple. No matter how hot it was, I should be focusing on Joel and the wedding.

"Why are you up so early?" The sound of Sab's voice startles me, and I bang my head on the wall.

"Shit," I hiss, rubbing the back of my skull. "You scared me."

"You were a million miles away."

"Just thinking."

"About?" she asks, climbing onto the seat across from me.

"Everything."

"Wanna talk about it?"

Looking over at my best friend, I know I can tell her anything and it will stay in the vault, but I can't discuss this with her. And it's not just because she doesn't know about

Maddox and me from years ago, it's because I'm ashamed of myself. Here I am lusting over another man and a faceless dream man when I have a fiancé who loves me unconditionally. So I go with the safe option of, "Just nervous about the wedding."

"I know the feeling," she says, and I know she isn't just saying that. I remember how jittery she was in the lead-up to her wedding. Eamon is her everything and from the moment those two hooked up, it was game over. They were each other's firsts and they will be each other's lasts. If two people were meant to be, it's Eamon and Sabrina. And I want that too. "You remember how nervous I was and, if I'm honest, the last two weeks before my wedding were hell."

"You never told me that. I knew you were stressed, but I didn't know it was hell."

"I hid that from everyone."

"Why?"

"I honestly don't know," she says. "I wanted more than anything to be Mrs. Eamon McMahon, but at times I felt like it was dragging. Then I made that stupid pact where we wouldn't sleep together before the big day, and I became this horny, ragey person."

"No wonder Bridezilla was so zilla-ey, you were in heat too."

"Right?" She laughs. "Whatever you do, do not take sex off the table before you marry Joel. You need that release, and we all know a good fuck does wonders for the soul."

"Where do you come up with this shit?"

"Facebook," she casually replies, and I can't help but chuckle.

"So what you're saying is I need to fuck Joel and then everything will be fine in the world once again?"

"You never know, and if it doesn't work, at least you got laid. Coffee?"

Without waiting for a reply, she jumps up and heads into the kitchen. Leaving me to ponder her words and maybe she's right. Joel and I just need some us time, but trying to lock him down at the moment is like trying to get The G-team not to gossip—aka impossible.

MY FIRST OFFICIAL day of work isn't until Monday, so I gave myself the weekend to get settled. I spent all day yesterday unpacking and with everything almost done, I collapse onto the sofa for a break. I start watching a new series on Netflix but I get bored with that; Netflix and chill isn't really my scene. I'm going stir-crazy being confined to my apartment, so I pull on my uniform and decide to head into the station and see if they need a hand.

From memory, Sundays are either slow going or every man and his dog is up to mischief, and with it being the silly season, I'm betting it's option number two.

"Morning, Sheriff," Dennis greets me as I walk into the station.

"Morning, Dennis. How are things?"

"Can't complain. How—" We're interrupted when a call comes in about a missing goat. Dennis chuckles as he takes down the details, and then he's off to look into the case of the missing goat. Once again, leaving me alone since Drew is out on patrol and it's Stan's weekend off. Getting used to small-town policing will be an adjustment, but it's one I'm looking forward to.

Amongst the unpacking yesterday, I came here and set up my office so I could hit the ground running on Monday. It didn't take long since I didn't have much to unpack, but I did move the furniture around after my sister mentioned the feng shui of my office would be off by having my desk where it was. Not that I will admit it to her, but the room did feel better after I shuffled things around.

After leaving the station, I stopped in at Sips for a coffee and then I headed back to my apartment to finish unpacking, while thinking about *her*. I know I need to stop it but Ruby Olsen is pretty unforgettable. She's the one who got away. The forbidden fruit, as they say. It's so cliché hooking up with your little sister's best friend, but as soon as her tongue slipped into my mouth, I was hooked. That Christmas when Reindeer and I snuck around was one of the best Christmases of my life, but then I left and lost my chance.

..."*What happens now?*" *Ruby asks, tracing her fingertip over my pecs. It's the early hours of the morning, and we've spent the last two hours hidden away in my apartment exploring each other's bodies.*

"*What do you mean?*"

"*Well, you're leaving tomorrow and I'll still be here till school goes back. What about ... us?*"

"*I ... I don't know.*" *My words hang in the air.* "*I never really thought of the future.*"

"*Ohh,*" *she utters.*

"*I don't mean it like that, I just mean...*"

"*We're sneaking around and your sister is my best friend and you don't live here and this is nothing more than a holiday fling and now that Christmas is over, so are we.*"

"Reindeer—"

"You know, apart from Pops, you're the only other person to call me Reindeer."

"You're the only person I know who has a red nose year-round."

"I hate it." She lifts her hand and covers her nose.

"It's adorable," I tell her, pulling her hand away. Leaning over, I place a kiss on the tip of her ruby—pun intended—red nose. "Everything about you is adorable."

"Like what?"

"Everything. You are adorably perfect, Reindeer, and I wish things could be different with us."

"Me too, Mad. Me too."

Now that I'm back, I really wish it were different. I hate that younger me left because older me still thinks she's adorably perfect, and I can't be thinking that. She's not mine.

She's Joel's.

And very soon she will be his wife.

I'm sitting at my desk when a call comes in about hooligans swimming naked in the lake. "I'll get right on that, Ms. Ruthven." Apparently, she was driving back into town from visiting her sister over in Kingsbury Point, and she noticed people swimming naked. I'm sure she's mistaken because it's the middle of winter, no sane person would go swimming in the lake, let alone naked, but then again, today is the warmest it's been in days.

Grabbing the radio, I let Dennis and Drew know I'm heading out to investigate. They both complain at missing out on the possibility of seeing naked chicks in the lake. I remind them it's December; it's cold enough to freeze your piss, and Ms. Ruthven didn't say it was chicks.

Grabbing my hat, I slip it on, lock up my office, and climb

into my cruiser to attend the call. When I get to the lake, I'm
shocked at what I find.

58

twelve

RUBY

"DARE," I choose, and as soon as the word passes my lips, I instantly regret it.

Sab and I are sitting in the hot tub, drinking margaritas and giggling like schoolgirls. The pitcher is nearly empty, as is the bottle of red Sour Puss we used for shots beside it, but I'm too comfortable to climb out and make more. Only our heads are above the water, because even though the temperature is warmer today than it has been, it's still winter and there's a slight chill in the air. Steam billows off the bubbly water, and condensation pours out of our mouths with each breath we take. The sensible thing to do would be to take it inside, but Sab and I are anything but sensible when we get together—plus, we have margarita-brain and we all know what tequila does to sense and sensibility.

Even though it's just the two of us, today has been great and exactly what I needed. It's reminded me of our high school days when we'd sleep over at each other's houses. Back then, we'd sneak wine coolers down to the boathouse and drink them quickly to get a buzz. Then we'd fall into fits of giggles while playing truth or dare, just like now.

Sab suggested we play it and I eagerly agreed because she always manages to make me laugh, but instead of chugging wine coolers quickly, we sipped on margaritas and did shots of Sour Puss.

Right now, my stomach hurts from laughing so much, and I'm well past tipsy. Our dares are getting more and more wild, and the one Sab just offered is the craziest one so far. "I dare you to jump naked into the lake."

"Are you crazy? It's fucking arctic out here and you want me to jump naked into the lake?"

"We've swum naked in the lake before," she throws back at me.

"Yeah, in the middle of summer and in the middle of the night. Right now, it's the middle of the day and it's December."

"Live a little, Rubes," she challenges, with a look that always makes me cave to what she wants. She knows I've never been one to turn down a dare, and I'm not about to start now. "Okay, fine. I'll do it—"

"Yay," she squeals, clapping her hands.

"But only if you do it too," I counter offer.

"That's not how this game goes."

"You join me or it's no deal." She stares across the hot tub at me. "Please?" I beg, pouting at my best friend. "You know you want to."

"I do not want to jump naked into the lake," she protests but from the smile on her face, I know she's full of shit. I eye her and then she cackles like a witch. "Okay, yeah, I do kinda want to do it. We can pretend we are at one of those Scandinavian bath thingies."

"You are fucking crazy—"

"And that's why you love me."

It's true. I love my crazy best friend with every fiber of my being. "Okay, let's do this. We can pretend we are at an exclusive Scandinavian bath, but if I die, my frozen naked ghost is going to haunt you forever."

"Deal."

Sitting up, I shiver when the frigid air hits my skin. "Fuck me," I hiss, dropping my shoulders back under the water. The alcohol has made me think it's warmer than what it actually is, but I'm committed now. Needing some liquid encouragement, I reach over the edge and take a sip from the nearly empty Sour Puss bottle before handing it to Sab. She empties the bottle, then she grabs the margarita pitcher and drinks straight from the jug. She takes a huge gulp and hands it over to me.

Chugging back what's left, I place the empty pitcher down and I look over to my best friend. "Okay, let's do this."

We each peel off our bikini and throw the discarded material over the edge. We look at one another and begin to count. "One. Two. Three." On three we each jump up out of the water, climb out, and hand in hand we race down to the lake. Our feet pad across the icy dock, and me being me, I slip onto my ass. Sab cackles like a bitch but offers me her hand. Once I'm upright, we make our way to the end and before I chicken out, we leap.

There's no going back now.

Sailing through the cold frigid air, we crash into the water with an almighty splash. It feels like a million pins are stabbing me, and when I break the surface, I'm no longer holding Sab's hand. Treading water, I look around for her but I can't see her. Panic begins to build, but then her head pops up and she gasps for air.

"Holy fucking fuckballs," she breathlessly pants. "It's fucking cold."

"Understatement of the fucking century, Sab." My teeth are chattering, and my skin is burning from how cold it is.

"I dare you to climb out and cannonball in," she says.

"It's my turn to give you a dare," I tell her.

"I partook in your dare, therefore I get two in a row."

"What if I choose truth?"

"Okay, truth. If you could run away with anyone in the world, famous or otherwise, who would it be?"

"Okay, I'll cannonball in."

"You chickenshit." She splashes me and I laugh.

"Okay, well then, to sweeten the cannonball deal, after this, I will cook you my famous lobster mac and cheese."

"With New York cheesecake for dessert?"

"Deal," I agree.

After shaking her hand, I swim over to the dock and lift myself up. "Fuck me. It's even colder when you get out," I hiss.

You'd think with the sun shining and not a cloud being in the sky, it would be warmer than it is. And I guess it is, if you're not naked and swimming in the lake. The chatter of my teeth increases, and I'm just about to leap back in when Sab calls out, "If you do a sexy naked dance before jumping in, I will send you a case of wine a month for the next three months."

"Make it six months and you have a deal."

"Fine," she relents.

Taking a deep breath, I hum along to "Closer" by Nine Inch Nails, and I begin to shake my booty and seductively—well, I hope it is—dance on the dock while freezing my tatas off. After dropping down to a squat, I leap back into the water. Once again gasping when I come up, now I'm not sure what's colder, being in the water or being out.

"Oh my God," Sab says with a giggle. "That was the best."

"It was actually fun," I tell her.

"Really?"

"Really-really."

Before I know it, Sab climbs out and does a little dance and then jumps back in. When she surfaces, she's laughing like a hyena but agrees it was fun. Then we decide on a duet. We both climb out. We're singing a Backstreet Boys song when we hear the sound of a police siren.

My eyebrows raise, and I look to my best friend. She looks sheepish, and then with a giggle, she utters, "We are so fucked," before we jump back in to cover our nakedness from the law here to arrest us.

thirteen

MADDOX

DRIVING ALONG THE ROAD, I see a naked figure on the end of a dock before they jump into the water. Then another figure appears and after doing a little dance, they too jump back into the water. "The cold weather has brought out the crazy people," I mutter to myself as I pull into the driveway and when I see where I am, I shake my head and hold back a smirk.

Rolling down the driveway toward Tweedle Naked One and Tweedle Naked Two, I continue to shake my head as I watch my sister and her best friend frolic naked on the dock. Flicking on the siren, they both turn toward me. Shock is written all over their faces, and I chuckle to myself as I turn off the engine.

Pulling my hat on, I climb out of the car and hear splashes. The girls have jumped back into the lake to cover their nakedness. Opening the trunk, I grab out two blankets and walk toward the dock. "Really? Skinny-dipping?" I call out. "In this weather?"

"I dare you to join us," Sabbi calls out, ignoring the fact she's naked in the daylight or that I'm in my uniform.

"Sabrina." I use her full name to hopefully reiterate the seriousness of the situation. "I'm the new sheriff. I can't just go skinny-dipping on a Sunday afternoon."

"Chicken," she goads, and then Reindeer starts flapping her arms up and down while making chicken clucking sounds. Soon both of them are squawking like chickens. My sister knows I never back down from a dare … but I'm on the job.

"Sab, I'm working—"

"Don't you officially start Monday?" Reindeer asks. "'Cause, if so, technically, you aren't working-working, which means you can accept the dare."

Then my sister adds, "And if you don't, you will forever be known as a chicken."

And once again, they start with the clucking sounds.

Staring down at the two lunatics swimming in the freezing water, something inside of me snaps when Reindeer stares intently at me and mouths the words, "I dare you." That challenge snaps my restraint, and I begin to unbutton my shirt. Dropping it to the dock, I kick off my shoes and socks. Popping open the button on my trousers, I lower the fly and push my pants down. Standing on the dock in nothing but my briefs, I stare down at the girls. "Turn around," I tell them.

"I've seen your dick before," Sabrina states.

"Yeah, when I was like five," I snap. "Now turn around so I can complete my dare."

"Fine," she hisses and spins around. "You too, missy," she says to Reindeer. "You're about to be married, and there's only one dick you should be staring at."

"If you've seen one dick you've seen them all," she says to my sister.

"I disagree. Some are long and thin. Some look like little toadstools. Some are thick and girthy. Some are circumcised, while others are not. Some are pierced. Some—"

"For someone who's only been with one guy, you sure know a lot about them," Reindeer teases her.

"It's called porn, Ruby, and you should know; you sell it daily."

"I don't sell porn. I sell romantic experiences that just so happen to feature men with gorgeous long dicks and they know how to bring a girl to her knees with said gorgeous and long dick."

Having had enough of hearing my sister and her best friend talk about male anatomy, I lower my briefs and jump before I can talk myself out of this stupid idea. Holy fucking coldness, Batman, I knew the water would be chilly but I wasn't expecting it to be this cold. "Fuck me sideways," I splutter when I surface.

"Takes your breath away, huh?" Reindeer says, splashing me.

"That's the understatement of the century," I tell her. "Now, wanna tell me how you two ended up skinny-dipping?"

"Well, we were in the hot tub drinking and doing shots and then one thing led to another, and well, here we are."

"Only you two would end up doing this."

"Umm, hello, didn't you and Chris Douglas do exactly this in your senior year?" At the mention of Chris, I smile. I haven't thought of him in years. Maybe now that I'm back, we can reconnect and we can start when I pick my truck up from him. I was lucky all I did was bust the radiator when I crashed 'cause this time of year, it's hard to get parts and I hate the rental I have. I can't wait to get my truck back.

"That was in the past. I'm the sheriff now. I need to be responsible."

"So responsible that at the goading of your sister and her best friend, you stripped and jumped into the lake," Reindeer states matter-of-factly.

"Shut up," I throw back at her before I splash her.

"So tough," she taunts.

"I'll show you tough." Before she can process what I'm up to, I have my arms around her waist, my hand brushes the underside of her breast, and as I lift Reindeer into the air, it hits me she and I are naked ... with my sister. At that thought, I quickly throw her into the water.

"Asshole," she coughs when she resurfaces.

Shrugging at her, I waggle my eyebrows at her and then it's on. She launches herself at me, and before I know it, she's on my back, trying to dunk me. She pushes herself up on my shoulders and tries to push me under, but I'm too strong for her, and she slips down my back. Her naked breasts slide over my skin, and I can feel her tight and taut nipples grazing me. They are stiff and pebbled from the cold—hard enough to cut steel.

Sliding my arm behind me, I tug her around me and my cock brushes against her stomach, at the realization I'm naked, she pushes off of me but not before her eyes widen. We stare intently at one another, each of us breathing heavily and I'm not sure if it's from the exertion of our play fighting or something more.

The moment, however, is interrupted when Sabrina calls out, "Cannonball," just before her ball-shaped body crashes into the water, soaking Reindeer and me.

An all-out water fight breaks out. The three of us are splashing each other and trying to dunk one another. Even though it's colder than a witch's tit, I can't remember the last time I had this much fun ... even if what we're doing at the moment is illegal.

We all take turns cannonballing and splashing, with a rule of "no looking." I'm happy to oblige when it's my sister's turn, but I will admit, I sneak a peek or two when it is Ruby's turn.

Her body is just as lithe and stunning as I remember. Her arms are toned and her stomach is flatter than a pancake.

"Well, well, well," a deep voice sings out, "What's going on here?"

When I look up to the dock, my eyes widen when I see Deputy Drew standing there with his hands on his hips and a shit-eating grin on his face. If I thought crashing my car upon my arrival was embarrassing, being caught naked with your sister and her best friend in the lake, well, that's a whole other level of embarrassment.

fourteen

RUBY

MY BODY FREEZES and my heart literally stops at the sound of a deep, masculine voice behind me, "Well, well, well. What's going on here?" We are so fucked, and not in the good way when you're naked. Right now, all I can think about is I'm about to be arrested for being naked in public. Meaning, I'll be in jail on my wedding day, rocking an orange jumpsuit and not my gorgeous gown. Speaking of clothes, I'd really like mine right about now.

Turning my head, I look toward the dock and I see two feet clad in black boots. Ever so slowly, I trace my gaze up and when I see who it is, a small gasp escapes me. Before us is Drew Westwood—Deputy Drew Westwood. He has a smug smirk on his face. "Thought you were here looking into hooligans swimming naked in the lake, I didn't realize *you* were the hooligan swimming naked in the lake."

"Is there any chance you can forget you saw this?" Maddox asks, swimming over to the dock. He rests his arms on the edge and stares up at his deputy.

"We can ... but it will cost you."

"What will your silence cost?" Maddox asks as he pulls

himself up and out of the water. Not showing an ounce of shame at flashing his dick to his deputy. If I wasn't mortified, I'd take the moment to appreciate his toned back and muscular ass—you could literally bounce a quarter off those glutes—but I need to focus on the mess we're in right now.

"Fuck, dude, put your junk away. Is that—"

"Deal," Maddox says, outstretching his hand to Drew.

"If it means you put that anaconda away, you have a deal."

"Excellent," Maddox replies with a nod before bending down and pulling his pants back on. Sliding his feet into his boots, sans socks, he then picks up his shirt, pulls one arm in, and looks down to Sab and me. "Ladies, I suggest you keep the skinny-dipping for after-hours so as to not traumatize the locals." He looks to Drew and hits him in the arm. "Hey, stop perving at my sister or I'll be forced to tell Georgie you were looking at another woman."

"I wasn't perving," he defends himself.

"Why not?" Sab calls out. "My tits are fabulous for having had two kids sucking on them." She pushes the girls together to perk them up, and I laugh when I see both Mad and Drew quickly avert their gaze and look the other way.

"Bye, ladies," Maddox says with a wave over his shoulder before shoving Drew to get moving. Drew follows Mad, not saying goodbye, but I think the poor man is traumatized right now.

"Oh my God," I cry out when they're gone. "I was sure we were going to be arrested."

"Please," Sab says. "My brother is the sheriff."

"So?"

"He's like, untouchable."

"This isn't television. He's subject to all the laws we are." How she is so calm after what just happened, I will never know. My heart is still racing. "Maybe we should head back inside."

"Yeah, I think we should. My vagina is going to freeze off, and I reckon my nipples could cut glass right now. They have never been this stiff before. Not even when Eamon and I tried ice play."

"I don't want to know about that." I scoff, splashing water at her.

"You really should try it. It's so fun and the orgasm afterward? In-fucking-tense."

"What makes you think I'm a kinky bitch?"

"Hello, you peddle porn for a living."

"I do not peddle porn! I sell romance novels."

"Potato. Vodka. Now, let's head inside. My buzz is wearing off and my—"

"Let's go," I interrupt before she can tell me about her vagina and nipples again.

Bringing out our inner Jennifer Garner in *Alias*, we sneak back up to the cottage and we make it back without seeing anyone. We each head to our room and when I close the door, I make a beeline for the shower. Turning the water on, I wait for it to heat up and when I step under the spray, the hot water burns my skin. It stings in a similar way to when I jumped into the lake but as my skin heats up, the pain dissipates.

Climbing out, I dry myself off and pull on a pair of yoga pants and a 'SMUT UNIVERSITY' sweatshirt I recently got into the store. With my fluffy socks in hand, I grab my phone and when I unlock it, I'm disappointed when I don't have a message from Joel. I haven't seen or heard from him since our lunch on Friday. I thought he'd at least text to say good morning or night, but there's nothing. I know I could text him, too, so I decide to do just that.

RUBY

Hey, Joel. Hope you're having a good weekend.
I've had a great time with Sab. It's just what I
needed with the chaos of final wedding prep
about to start. Love you Xo

Walking out to the living room, I find Sab in the kitchen. She's opened a bottle of red and she's started prepping her famous risotto for dinner—*looks like I'm off the hook for dinner but I will make cheesecake for dessert once she's done.* "If I was into chicks, I would totally marry you."

"And what's not to love?"

"Thank you," I tell her as I pull out a chair at the island and watch her.

"For what?"

"This weekend. Apart from almost getting arrested, it's been a blast and just what I needed."

"Well, I'm happy to do it. You're my sister from another mister, and there isn't anything I wouldn't do for you."

"Back at ya, lady."

Her mouth opens and closes, like she wants to say something else, but the timer on the oven snares her attention and the moment passes.

After finishing the bottle of wine while I whip up the cheesecake, Sab opens another while it's setting and then we spend the rest of the evening in front of the television, watching *Magic Mike* and *Magic Mike XXL*. The credits roll and when I look over at my bestie, I see her staring at me. "What?" I ask. "Do I have chocolate on my face?" She shakes her head. "Then what?"

"I want to say something but I'm not sure how you're going to take it."

"You can tell me anything," I tell her.

"I know but, well..."

"Spit it out, Whitworth."

"You haven't called me Whitworth since I married Eamon."

"You're stalling and, to be honest, you're scaring me."

"Okay, well, ummm, it's about Joel and you."

"Go on," I urge her but with how scared she is to tell me, I'm kinda scared too.

"Joel is a great guy and all that jazz, but are you sure he's the one?"

"Yes?" I reply but it comes out as more of a question than an affirmative answer. "Why do you say that?"

"He hasn't called you once this weekend. Eamon and I have spoken morning and night."

"But you have the girls," I remind her.

"We do, but I have also spoken to him and just him, but it's not just that. He hasn't done anything for the wedding. It's all been left up to you. The two of you don't even live together—" I go to interrupt her but she halts me with her hand. "And don't give me the 'we will after we get married' bullshit. Couples live together before they get married, this isn't the eighteen hundreds anymore. You and he don't have anything in common and need I remind you, on Friday, he bought you fungi soup. If that isn't a red flag, I don't know what it." She pauses. "I just want you to be sure he's what you want. You read all these stories about men who would die for their women and then you end up with Joel—the complete opposite."

"Joel's sweet and reliable and I can count on him."

"I never said you couldn't but tell me this, when he kisses you, does everything around you fade away? Does it feel like it's just the two of you? Because if that doesn't happen, he's not your penguin."

Sitting here, I process her words. I don't know what to say

because all the points she made are valid, but I love him. And love conquers all, right?

The next morning, I wave bye to Sab and she heads back to her family. I ask her to drop me off at home so I can pop a load of laundry in before I head into work. It's always busy this time of year with last-minute Christmas shoppers and with planning a wedding as well, I will be rushed off my feet.

Unlocking the front door, I step inside and head into my bedroom. Dropping my bag on the bed, I begin to unpack before I grab the laundry hamper, and I pop a load in.

Walking back into the living room, my gaze lands on the Christmas ornament Sab gave me. It really is beautiful, and I think about what the shopkeeper told her when she bought it. *The ornament is enchanted, and the person who receives it will be able to look into their future to find their true love.* "Okay, ornament, let's try again and see if you really are enchanted." Walking over to the tree, I cup the star in my palm. "Show me my true love."

DING DONG

My eyes widen at the sound of my doorbell. Walking over to the door, I swing it open and I'm surprised at who I see standing there.

fifteen

MADDOX

"MADDOX, WHAT ARE YOU DOING HERE?"

"Hey, Reindeer, I'm here on official police business." Her eyes widen, and immediately I think I know why she thinks I'm here. She thinks I'm here to arrest her over yesterday's skinny-dipping incident. As much as I want to tease her, seeing the sheer panic on her face is more than I can handle so I don't, especially when she lifts her wrists up and holds them out to me. "What are you doing?"

"Aren't you here to arrest me for what happened yesterday?"

"If I arrested you, I'd have to arrest my sister, as well as myself since the three of us were involved. Besides, I'm the sheriff, I'm pardoning us for our naked crimes."

"Isn't the president the only person who can pardon anyone?"

"President, sheriff. Same-same." She chuckles and bites her bottom lip as she lowers her arms down.

"Well, if you aren't here to arrest me, what *are* you here for?"

"There have been reports of someone leaving flaming bags

75

of shit on people's doorsteps in the area, was just checking to see if you've had this happen?"

"Ummm, well, I've been away all weekend, but no, I haven't had any deliveries like that."

"Okay, well, if that changes, please call it in. We want to catch the little turds."

"Will do, Sheriff." She laughs and smiles as she says this. She must notice the quizzical look on my face. "It's weird calling you Sheriff, but at the same time it's not because you were born for this. And I must say, you look damn good in that uniform."

"I look even better out of it," I tell her with a wink. Her cheeks darken and I'm accosted with an image of her naked and her whole body that color after I've made her climax with my tongue in her pussy and my finger in her ass. If memory serves me correctly, Miss Prim and Proper loves a little ass play ... with the right kind of lubrication. "I love that shade of pink on you, Reindeer ... especially after you come from my tongue in your pussy and my finger in your ass."

"Maddox," she hisses. "You can't say things like that, what if Joel was here?"

"It's Monday morning. At ten and he'll be at work. Besides, he doesn't live here."

"Not yet he doesn't, but after the wedding he will."

"I didn't know that." I hate the fact she's engaged to another man, and from what I know of Joel-fucking-Prior, a highlighter is brighter than him. The guys down at the station do not see what she sees in him. Stan thinks Joel has a monster cock and that's the only reason Reindeer is with him, but I know Reindeer, she wouldn't be with a guy just for his dick. There must be something special about him, *lucky bastard.*

"Well, now you do and if there isn't anything else, I need to get to work."

"Nope, nothing else, but if you do—"

"See anything, I'll let you know."

"Thanks. Have a good day, Ms. Olsen."

"You too, Sheriff Whitworth."

Nodding at her, I walk down the path and climb back into my cruiser. Sitting here, I make notes on the case. Not that there's much to go on and the sound of a car's engine garners my attention. When I look up, I see Reindeer backing out of the driveway. As she passes me, she waves and heads off to work.

It's funny. When I returned here and looked to the future, I saw myself settling down with her. Us living in a cabin up on the mountain. We'd drive into town together each day. We'd have lunch dates once a week, and we'd spend our Friday nights at The Reindeer Hole. Once we each had a buzz, we'd head home to our cabin and stay up all night ravishing each other.

Thoughts of what will never be are interrupted when the radio crackles to life and I'm asked to get back to the station ASAP due to a situation.

"Get fucked, you redneck weasel," a feminine voice screeches as I hang up my coat.

"Miss, I'm going to need you to calm down." My eyes widen when I hear Stan say that because everyone knows you never, *never*, tell a woman to calm down.

"What the fuck did you just say?" she bellows. "Don't you know who I am? I can have every single one of you redneck hicks fired an—"

"I thought we were redneck weasels," I state as I walk into the station.

"Same-sa—" The lady cuffed in holding stops mid-tirade when she looks to me. "Well, hello there, good-looking." Her eyes rake over me, and she licks her lips seductively.

Ignoring her, I focus on a panicked-looking Stan. "Want me to take over?"

"Please." He nods and before I can say anything else, he scurries over to me and away from the irate woman in holding.

"What seems to be the issue?" I ask my deputy.

"The issue," the woman shouts, "is your incompetent deputy has charged me with a DUI."

"Have you been drinking?"

"Well, yeah, but like, I only had six mimosas at breakfast and maybe a bottle and a half of chardonnay."

"It's ten in the morning?" She just shrugs. I turn to Stan. "Tell me what went down."

"I was out on patrol and I followed her as she left Lake's Edge Motor Lodge. She was weaving all over the road so I pulled her over. Did a roadside sobriety test and she failed. Then she blew point one nine-nine and I promptly charged her," Stan tells me. "Now she's refusing to cooperate."

I look to the woman. "Miss—"

"You can call me, Jess," she purrs.

"Name's Jess Hammerson. Forty-five and from Las Vegas." He steps closer to me and lowers his voice. "System shows this is her third offense."

Nodding at Stan, I turn to face our guest. "What brings you to Evergreen Lake?" I ask her.

"None of your fucking business," she hisses, then in the blink of an eye, she purses her lips and looks at me. She's going for seductive, but it's anything but. "Maybe over a drink we could get to know one another better."

"I think you've had enough for all of us, Ms. Hammerson, but from what my deputy is telling me, he's well within his right to have arrested you. As this is your third strike, you're looking at a Class B felony with jail time."

"It was only a couple of drinks," she pleads, her eyes welling with tears.

"A couple of drinks is two, Ms. Hammerson. Last time I checked, six mimosas and a bottle and a half of chardonnay is more than that. You could have seriously injured yourself or someone else. We take the safety of this town seriously, and your actions put that safety at risk."

"But—"

"Nope," I interrupt her. "No buts. I've seen firsthand the devastation a drunk driver can cause, and I will not have you ruining someone's Christmas. Here's what's going to happen, you're going to let Stan process you, and then you'll be taken over to the courthouse because lucky for you, the judge is in today. He will make his ruling and that'll be that. And just so you know, he lost his wife to a drunk driver."

Her eyes widen and tears streak down her cheeks, but I can tell from the look in her eyes that she's not sorry for her actions, she's just sorry she got caught.

Looking to Stan, I nod at him and he smiles. I watch on as she finally follows Stan's directive, and before we know it, he's escorting her over to the courthouse. A call comes in, seems we have another flaming poop incident to investigate.

My first official day on the job is off to a busy start, but I'm loving it. It's Christmas and I have the best job in the whole damn world.

sixteen

RUBY

PULLING INTO MY GARAGE, I let out a yawn. The weekend with Sab was perfect in every way, but I'm too old to drink till the wee hours … or go skinny-dipping in early December. My nipples are still frozen, but frozen nipples aside, it was just what I needed but at the same time, now I'm confused.

My chat with Sab has been all I can think about, and her question, "Are you sure he's the one?" has really thrown me—because I do love Joel, but am I *in* love with him? In all the books I read, when the female main character is about to walk down the aisle, she knows with every fiber of her being the man at the other end is her one true love. Up until a few days ago, I was sure, but now I'm so fucking confused.

Grabbing my handbag from the passenger seat, I head inside, no closer to knowing what I want but one thing is abundantly clear, Joel and I need to talk. We used to talk all the time, but lately, apart from a text message here and there, we hardly speak anymore.

Pushing open the door from the garage into the kitchen, I stop mid step and gasp. Standing before me with a massive Christmas-inspired flower arrangement is Joel. In the background, Christmas music is softly playing and warmth from the fire hits me square in the face.

"Hi, Rubes," he greets, walking over to me. Leaning into me, he cups my cheek and presses his lips to mine. And just like the first time he kissed me in college, my eyes drift closed and my heart skips a beat. This kiss is soft, sensual, and ohh so perfect. My romance-loving heart is swooning right now.

"Hi," I whisper against his lips before he kisses me deeply again. My swoon level increases when he rests his forehead against mine and we stand here, silently gazing into each other's eyes. "What's all this?"

"Life has been crazy lately and after having lunch with you on Friday, I realized I missed you so I did this for you." He waves his hand around, and when I peek over his shoulder, I see the lights in my place are dimmed and my living room has been turned into a movie theatre. It looks like every pillow, blanket, and duvet in my place has been pulled out to create a bed just for two. On the coffee table is a bucket of popcorn, a bowl of Skittles, and a wine bucket with a bottle of what I hope is prosecco.

Joel is grinning like a carnival clown when I look back at him, and I find myself smiling too.

"You did this for me?"

He nods. "Mmmhmpf. I also need to apologize."

"Why?" I ask, confused.

"On Friday, I gave you the wrong soup at lunch. You know I can't pass up Norah's mushroom soup, but I was so hungry I didn't even realize until I got into my car and was halfway back to work that I ate both the chicken noodle and the mushroom one."

"I was wondering about that."

"I'm so sorry. I'm a shitty fiancé, so this is my way of making it up to you."

"Well, you're off to a good start but if there is one mush-room in sight, I might have to call off this wedding."

"I assure you, there are no mushrooms ... well, I hope there aren't. I cannot take credit for the meal."

"And what meal might that be?"

"Pizza," he says proudly. "Pepperoni with olives for you and cheese for me."

"I will never get why you love that so much, it's so ... plain."

"What can I say? I'm a plain kind of guy."

"Lucky for you, I like plain guys."

"Only *like*?" he teases.

"Maybe I love ... a little ... I mean, you do love mushrooms."

"Well, I love you—olives and all."

That's kinda sweet, I think to myself. He tells me to go get changed and he'll pour me a glass of prosecco—I was right—and bring up the movie, *Top Gun: Maverick.*

Joel and I have a lovely night together, eating pizza and watching the movie. Not that we see much because we make out like teenagers. The movie is finished and we're lying here in each other's arms, watching the flames of the fire flicker. He leans down and kisses me. It's getting hot and heavy when he suddenly pulls away. He then shocks me when he bids me a good night, making a promise to see me Wednesday to do wedding prep.

He kisses the tip of my nose and lets himself out. Leaving me lying here in the makeshift bed confused, alone, and horny. How can we go from hot and heavy kisses and petting to nothing?

Standing up, I begin to pack up the bedding. Right now, I'm pissed off and even more confused than before. Yes, he apolo-gized for the soup debacle from Friday, but he left without giving me an orgasm. A hero in my book wouldn't do that. Before he left, he'd fuck me into next week, leaving me completely sated and possibly waddling the next day. Placing the last cushion back on the sofa, I drop down into the chair when it hits me: I can't remember the last time we were intimate together. There's been kisses, hot and heavy kisses, and a blow job in his car after meeting at the lodge to finalize the dinner menu for the wedding, but actual intercourse? It's been months. Why doesn't my fiancé want to sleep with me?

seventeen

RUBY

A FEW DAYS LATER, I'm in Hanson's Mercantile, the local grocery/bakery/post office/anything you can think of store, doing my weekly grocery shopping when my phone rings. I smile when I see Joel's name flashing on the screen. He and I have been playing phone tag all day, so I'm excited we can finally chat.

Joel and I are meeting up tonight so we can finish putting together the thank-you baskets for our bridal party. He got personalized beer mugs for his groomsmen, and for my only bridesmaid, a champagne flute and a satin robe. All of them will get a care package that consists of headache pills, water, energy drinks, and snacks to keep them going on what's sure to be a busy day. I'm still worried the photos will be off because I only want Sab by my side whereas Joel has three groomsmen, his brother and two friends, but when push came to shove, I didn't want to add people just to even things out. Joel assures me it will all be fine because people will be focused on me, but I'm still worried.

"Hey hey, fiancé," I say when I answer. I love saying fiancé but I cannot wait until I get to call him my husbutt. I decided on husbutt because Joel has a sexy butt. It's tight and muscular for an accountant, and was one of the things I first noticed about him.

"Hey, Rubes."

"I'm just at the store, I should be home in a few but you can let yourself in and get started if you want, and then I can start on dinner and then—"

"I'm not coming," he states, interrupting me. His tone gives nothing away but it causes me to stop in the middle of the aisle. I rapidly blink as I process his words. "What do you mean, you're not coming?" I hiss into the phone.

"I have to get this report done and I'm behind."

"Joel," I plead. "We need to get this done, we're getting married—"

"That's all you talk about," he snaps, interrupting me. "Wedding this. Wedding that. There's more to life than the wedding."

"Are you shitting me right now?" I shout. "You have done shit all for *our* wedding, and I thought we could at least do this together, since it's for those helping *us* on our special day."

"Like that matters, besides, everyone knows weddings are for the chick."

"You did not just say that to me." The gall of this man. Weddings are the union of *two* people who love each other unconditionally and want to spend the rest of their lives together. Yes, the woman has a pretty dress, but the guy has a tux and his hair styled. It's about both of us, and he knows that because he has just as much of a say in things as I have. If anything, I've given in to him at every turn. My dream had always been to get married by the lake, surrounded by snow before we moved into a tent for the reception. It'd be lit by millions of fairy lights and tea light candles would sit on high-top cocktail tables. Gas heaters would provide warmth since it was winter. Waiters would continually walk around with trays of finger foods and drinks. There'd be no sit-down dinner so people could mingle and have fun.

"It's true," he states. "Look, I'll pop by later this week and we can do it then if you don't have it done, but I really need to get this report finalized and submitted before the holidays."

"I—" Before I can finish my sentence, he hangs up.

He.

Hangs.

Up.

No "I love you" or "Talk soon."

Just the dial tone.

My eyes well with tears and when I look up, Delivery Dan is staring at me. Great, this is all I need because now, by tomorrow morning, the whole town is going to know Joel and I had a fight over the phone. Smiling at him, I spin around, my cart narrowly missing the shelving before I race away from him. My vision blurs as I storm down the aisle. I will the tears to stay away and so far, they comply. I turn the corner without watching where I'm going and I crash into another cart. When I look up, I see Maddox. He smiles but when he notices my tear-filled expression, his smile disappears. "Reindeer, what's wrong?"

That question causes the dam to break and the tears begin to fall like an avalanche down my cheeks. In the middle of Hanson's, I break down. The next thing I know, I'm in Maddox's arms. He's consoling me without knowing what caused the waterworks.

Wrapping my arms around his waist, I burrow in and let all my grief out. I thought Joel and I had turned a corner. The other night was magical in every way. It reminded me of the Joel from when we first started dating. Finally, he and I were on the same page but, clearly, I misread things because it's obvious his job is more important than me.

GROCERY SHOPPING IS my least favorite pastime, along with folding the laundry and cleaning the toilet. My aversion to doing the groceries sucks because I love to cook. On the way home from the station, I had a craving for chicken Alfredo and surprise, surprise, my refrigerator and pantry are empty when I check them. In my defense, I only moved in a few days ago, and I've been busy ... lusting over a blond bookstore owner, who's about to marry another man.

As much as I love the food at the various food places in town, I'm craving home-cooked meals, so I quickly put together a meal plan for the next week. Then I write a shopping list of all the foods I'll need. Forty minutes later, here I am, spending my evening in Hanson's Mercantile pushing a shopping cart around. This place has been here since the dawn of time. The floorboards underneath my feet creak with every step I take. When I was little, I used to think the floor was going to give way and since this place has been here forever, I'd fall into a secret dungeon down below. It would either be filled with skeletons or a long-lost treasure, just like in *The Goonies*. Thankfully, the flooring has never given out and I'm still unaware of any skeletons or treasure hidden below the building.

The cafe here, Granny Taught Us How, sells the best old-fashioned donuts. I know it's cliché for a police officer to like donuts, but these doughy little rounds of bliss are worth the teasing wrath and stereotype.

I've just about got everything on my list—which is surprising because the range here isn't as large as Kroger's or Whole Foods. I'm turning into the last aisle when someone comes around the corner and slams their shopping cart into me. I hate when people don't take care coming around the corner. I'm about to let loose on them but the words die on my lips when I see Reindeer is the person who crashed into me.

A smile appears on my face, but it quickly fades when I see she's upset. "Reindeer, what's wrong?" No sooner do those three words pass through my lips and she starts to cry. Without thinking, I wrap my arms around her and she sobs into my chest, her shoulders shaking up and down as she falls apart in my embrace. Did someone die? What's caused her to be so upset?

Her body continues to shudder in my arms as she lets it all out.

Whispering sweet nothings into her ear, I rub my hand up and down her back in a soothing motion. Well, I hope it's soothing. I'm going to go with yes, it is, because her shaking has stopped and I think she's no longer crying.

She lifts her head up and I stare at her tear-stained face. Running my thumbs under her eyes, I wipe away the last of her tears. "Reindeer, what's got you so upset?"

"He cancelled," she mumbles, dropping her gaze to the floor.

"Who cancelled?"

"Joel."

"He canceled the wedding?"

"No." She shakes her head. "He was supposed to come over for dinner tonight and then we were going to work on the bridal party thank-yous, but some stupid report is more important and now he's not coming."

Without thinking, I offer, "I'm happy to help."

"I can't ask you to do that."

"You aren't asking, I'm offering. Not that I know what to do, but how about I cook dinner while you work on the thank-yous?"

"I can't ask—"

"As I said, you didn't ask; I'm offering. And if it will sweeten the deal, I was planning on cooking chicken Alfredo tonight, and I know it just so happens to be a favorite of yours."

"I'm supposed to be clean eating so I can fit into my wedding dress."

My eyes run over her body and there's not an ounce of fat on her, even if there was, who cares? Size is just a number. It's what's on the inside that counts, and Reindeer is perfect, inside and out.

"For the record, you look perfect to me," I tell her. "Besides, we all need a cheat meal from time to time, and a creamy pasta with chicken is the best cheat meal, if you ask me."

"I've been cheating lots lately because Christmas always has the yummiest of foods, and gingerbread just so happens to pair well with a nice zinfandel."

"Zinfawhat?"

"Zinfandel, it's a red wine."

"Of course, you know about all the fancy wine varieties."

She laughs and hearing that after how I found her makes me smile on the inside. Now to get *her* to smile on the outside.

"Now that you're back in town, you will have to join our Wi-ook club."

"Wi-ook club?"

"Wine and book—Wi-ook." My head nods as I make the connection. "We meet every month on the second Thursday."

"When's the next Wi-ook club?" I ask, all the days are blurring into one, and I'm not sure if it's passed already or not.

"Tomorrow night," she tells me.

"I'll pencil it in," I tell her and then she smiles. A super bright Reindeer smile. She really is beautiful when she smiles, even with tear tracks on her face. "So, what do you say about my offer of dinner and help?"

"Well, a girl cannot pass up chicken and pasta and cream."

"So you only want me for my food?"

"Exactly."

"Well, I have to drop this off at home and then I'll be over."

"Sounds like a plan, Maddox. Thank you."

"No need to thank me. It's in my DNA to help, and whenever a pretty girl is crying, I must turn that frown upside down."

"That you did." She brushes a tendril of her golden-blond hair behind her ear, and I have to resist the urge to cup her cheek and kiss her. "I'll see you soon."

Nodding, I stand and watch her walk away. She turns the corner and I stand here, staring in the direction she just went when I feel a presence beside me, or should I say presences, plural. When I turn my head, I see the G-team standing there. "Ladies," I offer in greeting.

"You have less than two weeks," Sheila says, holding up two fingers, waving them in my face.

"Two weeks till what?"

"Till you'll have lost her forever," Mildred answers.

"What?" I hiss. "Lost who?"

"Ruby," Bernice states, shaking her head like I know what they're talking about.

"What are you talking about?"

"Men," Mildred states. Now it's her turn to shake her head. "You have less than two weeks to convince her that you're her true love."

"But we're just friends—"

"Please," Bernice interrupts. "You two have been gaga for one another since that Christmas you were sneaking around together." My eyes widen at her statement, and I open my mouth to protest but she presses her index finger to my lips. "Don't deny it, Sheriff. The three of us know everything that happens in this town."

"Everything," Mildred repeats.

"We even know things before they happen," Shelia adds.

"Mmmhmpf," I reply with a nod and, if I'm being honest, I believe them. These three are like oracles. Oracles of gossip, but gossiping aside, if you need anything, they'll be one of the first ones there and if they can't help, they'd find someone who can. "Make sure with dinner tonight, you take her some gingerbread cookies, they are her fave and they pair well with zinfandel."

"So I've heard and, ladies, as much as I would love to stay and chat, I have somewhere to be."

"Don't let us hold you up, Sheriff," Mildred says. "But remember what we said. Two weeks."

"Goodbye, ladies." With a nod of my head, I leave the G-team … and make my way to the liquor aisle to grab a bottle of zinfandel. With the wine in hand, I head to the checkouts.

Racing home, I drop off my groceries and then I get back into my rental car and drive over to Reindeer's to cook her dinner and help with the thank-yous.

Pulling into her driveway, I turn off the engine. Climbing out, I pop the trunk and grab the grocery bag. I cannot wait to get my truck back; I make a mental note to call Chris in the morning and see when it'll be ready. As I walk toward the front door, the G-team's words play over in my mind, but I shake the thoughts away because I lost Reindeer years ago. It doesn't matter there's still two weeks till her wedding, she's engaged to another man and I will not be a cheater or make her one ... no matter how much I wish she were mine.

nineteen

RUBY

AFTER PUTTING MY GROCERIES AWAY, I jump into the shower to freshen up. I quickly shave my legs, shampoo my hair, and add the conditioner. While that does its thing, I soap up my body. My nipples are sensitive when I run my soapy hands over them, and a tingle begins to develop between my thighs. Tilting my head back, I begin to rinse the conditioner out and realize I'm nervous for tonight. I don't know why, it's just Maddox. He and I have had dinner plenty of times over the years so this is no different ... but it is. I'm starting to see him in a different light, again, but it doesn't matter because I'm marrying Joel. Plus, he and I had our shot when I was nineteen, and as amazing as it was, it just wasn't meant to be. A few weeks after I got back to college, I met Joel and the rest is history, until now. We just seem so far apart right now, but I'm sure once the stresses of the wedding and Christmas are over, he and I will find our groove again.

Everything will be fine and dandy, but why do I suddenly feel like I'm making the wrong choice?

I was so excited and happy, but ever since Maddox crashed back into town and my life, everything feels off.

Maybe I feel off because I haven't had an orgasm since my dream with the faceless man the other night. Now is as good of a time as any. Turning around, I lean against the tile wall and slide my hand down my body and between my thighs. Circling my clit, a moan slips free as the pressure begins to build. I badly need a release and now the fuse has been lit, there's no stopping it now. Pressing my finger into my slit, I push it inside myself and plunge it in and out. On every other stroke, I pull all the way out to play with my clit. With my other hand, I massage and caress my breasts. Squeezing my nipple, I drop my head back and give myself over to the pleasure.

"Yes," I pant as my release approaches.

Shuffling around, I lift my leg up onto the shower bench, opening myself up and allowing me to press two fingers into me. Hooking them around, I press on that magic spot deep inside and with a guttural groan, I cry out as my orgasm unleashes.

Goosebumps dot my skin and every nerve ending lights up as I ride out my release.

Dropping down onto the shower seat, I catch my breath. My chest heaves as I suck in oxygen after holding my breath while I came. When I come back to Earth, I rewash myself and then I climb out. Drying off, I pull on my panties and bra. Grabbing my moisturizer off the counter, I walk over to the window bench and sit down. Lifting my leg up, I rub cream into my newly shaved legs and massage my feet, letting out a moan when I hit *the* spot in the arch of my foot before slipping on my socks. Standing up, I step into my leggings and a Christmas sweater and sweep my hair up into a messy bun.

Putting the cream away, I walk out of my bedroom and head over to the dining table. I stop and stare at the mess before me. My eyes well with tears again, and the anger I have for Joel resurfaces. He should be here and I hate that he's not.

A knock at the door interrupts my pity party. Taking a deep breath, I wipe at my eyes and head over to open it. "Hey," I say in greeting, a shiver wracks through my body as a gust of wind blows behind Mad. "Shit, it's cold out there."

"It is winter," Maddox replies as he kicks off his boots in my entryway.

"Let me take that," I offer as he struggles to shuck off his coat.

"I got it." He smiles and somehow manages to remove his jacket one-handed and hang it up on the hook. "Where's the kitchen?"

"Follow me." He nods. Turning, I walk down the short hallway and I can feel his eyes on me.

"Nice tree," he says as he places the bag he was holding down on the kitchen counter.

"Thanks. I'm pretty happy with it."

"You should be. It's beautiful and I love the red-and-green theme you have going on."

"It's cliché going with red and green but there's something about the colors that scream Christmas, and this year I wanted it to be really Christmassy."

"I get that. I felt off until my decorations were up. It was actually the first thing I did after unpacking."

"So you still really love Christmas, huh?" I ask him, as I get out a pan and pot for him.

"Yep, what's not to love?"

A chuckle escapes me because he's not wrong. Christmas is my favorite time of year too, hence why I'm getting married at Christmas. From the snow—yes, I know I'm weird loving it—to the smells: cinnamon, peppermint, pine and pinecones, vanilla, chocolate, the scents are endless. Then there's family and friends coming together to enjoy a meal and the sharing of presents. It's a magical time of year, and no one can change my mind.

"You don't have to try and convince me, Mad. Now, what can I do to help?"

"Nothing, just sit your pretty little ass down, drink some zinfa-blah-blah, and chat to me while I work."

"I can do all of that. Would you like a glass of zinfa-blah-blah, as you call it?"

"I'll have a taste since I've never tried it before."

"Ohhh, I get to pop your zinfandel cherry."

"We seem to like popping each other's cherries," he says with a cheeky smile. My cheeks heat as I remember the moment he's referring to…

…Sab hit the mulled wine at the tree lighting festival hard tonight, and on an empty stomach, which was a recipe for disaster. After cleaning up her vomit-stained clothes, Maddox and I put her to bed. Once she's sound asleep, he offers to walk me home. Eagerly I nod and he offers me his hand. He laces our fingers together and pulls me out of Sab's room.

We sneak through the house, not wanting to wake Mr. and Mrs. Whitworth. He helps me into my jacket before he puts his on. We slip out the back door into the dark of night and, once again, he takes my hand. We walk across the yard and over to the gate next to the garage.

Maddox is staying in the room above the garage because his mom turned his old bedroom into a craft room, not thinking about when her son would come back to visit. He happily agreed to stay in the garage apartment, even if it's colder than hell up there this time of year.

Pulling on my hand, he stops us by the stairs up to his apartment and before I know what's happening, he's pressing me into the side of the garage and he's kissing me. Just like our kiss last night, he pushes his tongue into my mouth and I push mine into his. If I thought our last kiss was amazing, this one is fan-fucking-tabolous but as quickly as it starts, he stops.

He rests his forehead against mine, breathlessly panting. "Do you wanna hang out for a little longer?"

Nodding my head, I swallow deeply before he laces our fingers together and we make our way up the stairs to his apartment.

Unlocking the door, he flicks a light on and steps aside for me to enter. Brushing past him, I step inside. I've only taken a few steps when he grips my wrist and like downstairs, just before, he presses me into the wall beside the now closed front door and kisses me. Draping my arms over his shoulders, I pull him into me and deepen the kiss and our connection. Sliding his leg between mine, he rubs it against my pussy, applying pressure to my clit. A moan slips out of my mouth as I rub myself back on him.

"Please," I murmur against his lips.

"Please what, Reindeer?"

"I ..." But I don't finish my sentence; I'm embarrassed to ask for what I want. I'm embarrassed to admit I'm a virgin.

"Look at me," he demands.

Lifting my gaze to his, I stare into his chocolate-brown orbs and I fall deeper in lust with my best friend's older brother. Ever since our kiss last night, he's all I've been able to think about. Kissing Maddox is better than I ever imagined. "Tell me and I'll make it happen."

"I ... I want you to make love to me, but umm—"

"Umm, what?" he interrupts me.

"I'm a virgin," I whisper. I drop my gaze to the floor, unable to look at him to see his reaction at my confession.

Reaching out, he places his finger under my chin and lifts my head up. "I'd be honored to pop your cherry, Reindeer." His eyes widen and I start to panic he's changed his mind, but when he says,

"Shit, sorry, that wasn't very romantic. What I should have said is I'd be honored to be your first."

My heart turns to mush and I fall harder for him. This is it, I'm about to lose my virginity to the man I've been lusting over for years. This is a dream come true but at the same time, it can't be real so I ask him, "Really?"

He nods and smiles in that way that sets me ablaze. "And, Reindeer, I'm going to make it a moment you'll never forget."

My eyes widen at his declaration, but his words warm me from the inside out.

I'd always dreamed Maddox Whitworth would take my virginity, and my dream is about to come true, but I know him. He's going to make it even more memorable than I ever thought possible because that's the kind of person he is. He'd do anything for those he loves and right now, he's about to give me something I will remember forever.

"You're blushing," he says, the sound of his voice snaps me back to the present.

"I was just thinking about the night you popped my cherry."

"That was the night that started it all."

"Actually, when you kissed me beforehand was when it all started."

"You kissed me," he defends.

"Uhhh uh, you kissed me, Maddox."

"Well, let's agree to disagree. Now, you get the wine and I'll start on our dinner before we tackle the wedding thank-yous."

The mention of the wedding thank-yous is like being splashed with a bucket of freezing cold water. How can I be lusting over one man when I'm marrying another?

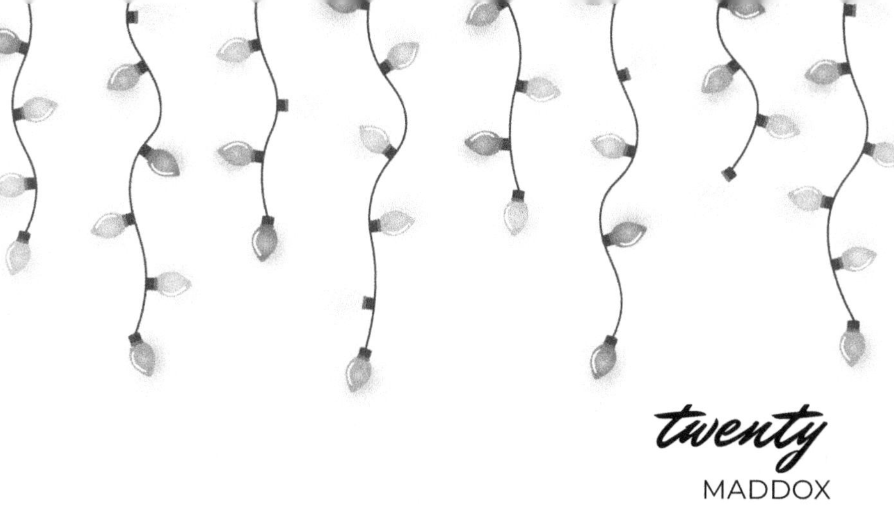

twenty

MADDOX

LAST NIGHT with Reindeer was fun, even if I was helping her put together thank-yous for her wedding ... to another man. I will always regret walking away from her but at the end of the day, I want her to be happy and it seems Joel is the man who makes her happy.

It's my turn to get coffees so I park my car and walk into Sips. Waving to the locals, I head to the counter and place my order with Syd. While I'm waiting, I hear "...they had a fight over the phone and then she was crying, in Sheriff Maddox's arms."

"Are they having an affair?" a feminine voice asks, pretty sure it's Ina, Stan's wife. She's currently nine months pregnant and due to give birth any day now. She's just as much of a gossip as the G-team, so I'm not surprised Delivery Dan is gossiping with her.

"If you ask me—" Delivery Dan speaks, but I interrupt him.

"It's none of your business." The sound of my voice causes Delivery Dan and Ina to turn toward me, shock written all over their faces. "You two should know better than to spread rumors like that. Reindeer is a family friend, and I was consoling her when she was upset."

"But why was she upset?" Ina excitedly asks, she waddles closer to me, resting her hand on her bump.

"That's between her and Joel."

"Are they splitting up? Is the wedding still on? Is he cheating? Or is she?"

"Yes, it's still on, and I'm not answering the rest because I don't gossip. But for what it's worth, couples argue all the time, don't they, Ina? And just because they do, it doesn't mean they are splitting up." Her face blanches at my words. The other day, I caught her and Stan arguing over names. They can't decide on a baby name and it was getting heated. I diffused the situation by telling them they should call the baby Cletus if it's a boy, or Wilma if it's a girl. Stan was not impressed but I personally think Wilma Wolensky has a great ring to it, if it's a girl. My interfering worked because the two of them got over their tiff and before Ina left, they made out like teenagers on prom night ... Stan later informed me orgasms help bring on labor, so I'm guessing they did more than just kiss.

"I better be going," she offers, and she quickly, well as quickly as you can when you're nine months pregnant, waddles out of Sips, and Delivery Dan gets back to his deliveries.

"You sure put them in their place," Sydney states, handing me my tray of to-go coffees.

"The gossiping here is one thing I will never get used to."

"I hear it all but sometimes the gossip is actual fact, and other times, it's so farfetched you'd think it was part of a television comedy. The one time, Sheila was convinced Mayor Sanchez had been replaced by a cyborg robot is a favorite of mine."

"What on earth made her think that?"

"Who knows, and I didn't ask. It's best that I just stand by, listen, and serve, otherwise, I'd never get any work done."

"Sounds like a good plan to me, have a great day, Syd."

"You too, Sheriff."

With my coffees in hand, I wave bye and head out to my car. A shudder racks through me when I stare at my rental. Being a small town, all the rental company had was a Kia Soul, a soccer mom's car and I'm no soccer mom. I cannot wait to get mine back. Which reminds me, I need to call Chris and follow up on when it'll be ready. Climbing in, I place the coffee tray on the passenger seat. Starting the car, I put it into gear and drive around to the station. Walking in, I deposit the drinks on everyone's desk and take a seat in my office, just as Stan arrives late, again. That man will be late to his own funeral.

He marches into my office. "What did you say to Ina? She just called me in tears."

"I didn't say anything to her."

"Clearly you did. She's distraught you told them she and I were fighting."

"I did no such thing," I defend myself. "And if you must know, she and Delivery Dan were speculating about Reindeer and Joel breaking up 'cause they had an argument. I just reminded her that couples fight from time to time."

"But why is she crying?"

"Stan, she's nine months pregnant with your sixth child."

"What's that got to do with it?"

"She's hormonal and emotional, didn't you say she cried the other day because when she sliced up the pie, it wasn't even and she didn't want to upset anyone?"

"Well, yeah, I guess. I just hate seeing, well, hearing her upset."

"Why don't you swing by home when you head out on patrol and make sure she's okay?"

"Are you sure?"

Nodding, I smile at my deputy. "Of course. Family always comes first."

"Thanks, Mad, appreciate it."

Stan grabs his coffee from his desk and heads back out, leaving me alone and wondering where Drew is. Calling him on the radio, he tells me he's investigating another flaming poop incident and he'll be back soon.

Leaning back in my chair, I sip on my coffee and chuckle when I think about our flaming poop offender. It has to be a kid because no adult would do that, but then again, if they're on drugs, anything is possible.

My cell rings and I pull it out. It's a local number I don't recognize but I answer it. "You've got Maddox."

"Maddox, it's Chris, your truck is ready."

"That was quick," I tell him.

"I knew you'd want it back ASAP after I saw you driving through town the other day in your soccer mom car." He chuckles. "I definitely think your truck is more suited to you."

I laugh too because he's right. "I'm on shift till four, can I swing by then?"

"I can drop it to you just after lunch, if that suits you?"

"That would be perfect, Chris. Send me the invoice and I'll fix you up."

"Will do. Catch ya later."

Smiling, I lean back in my chair. It's going to be a good day because I get my truck back and tonight it's Wi-ook club.

twenty-one

RUBY

I'VE JUST FINISHED SETTING up for Wi-ook club, and I smile because I have a surprise for the club this month. An author I absolutely love, Nicole Sanchez—no relation to our current mayor—sent us all copies of the first book in her *Love in the Big Apple* series. She also sent me a box of books for the store too, hence why I made her this month's featured author. Each month, I feature a new author. Last month was Cassie Laelyn and next month, I'm hoping to feature Rebecca Barber. If things work out, she's going to come visit and attend Wi-ook club in person, and that's amazing because she's from Australia and it's like eleventy billion miles away from Evergreen Lake.

The bell above the door chimes and when I walk into the main room, I smile when I see Maddox standing there. "You came," I utter.

"I said I would. I wasn't sure what time it started but I took a guess that it'd be six."

"Close, it starts at six thirty."

"Ohh, well, I'll come back then."

He turns to leave and I call out, "Don't go."

He looks at me over his shoulder. "You sure?" My head nods

on its own accord. "Okay," he agrees. Spinning around, he walks into the store and over to me. Leaning down, he places a chaste kiss on my cheek. "Hi," he whispers.

"Hi," I murmur back.

Standing here, we stare into each other's eyes. I'm accosted with a memory of staring intently into his, except in our memory, we're both naked in his bed, our legs entwined and my breasts pushed into his chest. The moment is broken when a car's headlights flash through the front windows of the store.

"Can I get you a drink?"

"Sure."

Walking away from him, he follows and when we step into the other room, he whistles appreciatively. "Wow, this is great." He walks farther into the space, and I watch as he takes it all in. Along the bar is an assortment of red and white wine, a jug of non-alcoholic Christmas punch, and platters of appetizers, both savory and sweet.

Since this is the last Wi-ook meeting of the year, I went all out. Normally it's just wine and cheese, but tonight we have all the trimmings—deli meats, fresh fruit, several different cheese varieties, crackers, nuts, and sweets, so many delicious sweets.

"It's not normally this flashy, but it's Christmas so I thought, why not?"

He joins me by the bar, and I hand him his glass of red. Our fingers brush and I feel a spark. It frightens me and I step back, tripping over the box of books for everyone. Before I end up on my ass, Maddox has his arms around me and he saves me from my imminent death, well, from falling over.

"I've got you," he purrs, well it sounds like he purrs and, once again, his hands rest on my hips and mine are on his chest. We stand here, precariously close. Our breaths mingle together as he holds me in his arms, the moment is interrupted when a throat clears.

Peering around Maddox, I see Joel standing there. "Joel!" his name squeaks out and I pull away from Maddox and walk toward Joel. "W-w-w-what are you doing here?" I stutter, my heart racing, but this time it's racing from guilt. Not that I have anything to be guilty about. Maddox just saved me from falling, nothing more.

"It's book and wine night," he says, pushing his hands into his pockets. "I thought I'd come."

"B-b-but you d-d-don't r-r-r-read?" My nerves are causing my words to come out all wrong. My palms are sweating and there's a heat running up my neck.

"I know I don't, but you were so excited for tonight and I can see why."

"It's not like that, Joel," I defend. Reaching out, I rest my hand on his forearm.

"It looks like Nicole came through," he voices and it takes a few moments for my brain to catch up. He's referring to the books, not what he walked in on ... not that anything was going on. "The books you were so excited for arrived in time." He nods to the table with the books from Nicole and then he picks one up and scans the front and back before popping it back down.

"Ohhh," I utter. "Yeah, they came in late today, so it's been a mad rush to get everything ready for tonight." Joel nods but his gaze keeps flicking to Maddox hovering behind me. The atmosphere between the three of us is awkward, and I know Joel is thinking the worst. I'm just about to explain what he walked in on but before I can say anything else, the bell chimes.

Chatter filters through the air as the rest of the club start to arrive. I'm pulled away from Joel when one of the group, Mrs. Winters, starts asking me questions about her new favorite trope, why choose romance. She's talking about how amazing it would be to be ravished by three or more men at one time.

From behind us, Joel scoffs in disgust when she says, "Any hole is a goal."

Mrs. Winters's head snaps in his direction and she glares at Joel. "Do you have a problem with a woman liking erotica?" She's not one to hold back her thoughts, especially when it comes to her reading taste.

"It's not appropriate for a woman of your age to be reading stuff like that."

"And what's wrong with a sixty-nine"—she chuckles at the number—"year-old woman liking to read about a woman being ravished?"

"It's not appropriate," he reiterates.

She stares him down and before I can jump in, she places her hands on her hips and glares at Joel. "Opinions are like assholes, everyone has one and in this instance, your opinion is wrong. Now, if you excuse me, I need to not be near a small-minded man."

She turns and walks away from us, muttering to herself about uneducated people and who cares if she likes reading smut.

"That was rude," I whisper-hiss to Joel.

"I know she was," he snaps.

"I was referring to you."

"I was rude?" he growls. "She called me an asshole."

"Well, she wasn't wrong. Just because you don't like what she likes, doesn't make what she likes wrong."

"Don't tell me you read that drivel?"

"Yes, Joel, I do read it—and, newsflash—I love it just as much as Mrs. Winters. Ninety percent of the books in here are filled with schmexy ravishing scenes."

His mouth drops open in shock. "What has gotten into you?"

"What?" I ask, confused.

"You were never like this when we started dating."

"Joel, I was an English Lit major. I love love."

"That's not love, that's … wrong."

"That's your opinion, Joel. We don't judge you for reading spy thrillers, why judge us for reading romance?"

"Smut is not romance."

"Yes, it is," I shout and all other conversations in the store comes to a halt. Without looking over my shoulder, I can tell everyone is gazing at us. No doubt this fight will be all over town tomorrow, but I'm too angry to care right now. Joel is being a judgmental dick right now, and I don't want him here, ruining the fun atmosphere that is Wi-ook Club. Stepping closer to him, I lower my voice. "I think it might be best if you leave. You clearly have a different view from everyone here when it comes to books, and I don't want tonight to be awkward."

"I came to support you, but I can see you don't want my support."

"Support, yes. Judgement, no," I snap.

Silently we stare at one another, my words hang in the air. His head starts to bob up and down and then without saying anything, he turns on his heel and walks out of the store, slamming the door behind him.

Covering my mouth with my hand, I swallow back the sob wanting to break free.

A hand touches my shoulder and instantly I feel relief. Turning my head, I look into the concerned eyes of Maddox. "You okay, Reindeer?"

Swallowing, I nod and smile at him. Taking a deep breath, I plaster on a fake smile and with my head held high, walk to the front of the room.

"Let's get started."

twenty-two

MADDOX

"HAVE YOU SPOKEN TO RUBES RECENTLY?" Sabbi asks.

"Nope," I tell her. *But I have wanked off thinking about her every night since Wi-ook club.* "Why, what's up?"

"She seems … off."

"What do you mean by 'off'?" I ask, balancing the phone between ear and shoulder so I can stir my sauce before I throw the gnocchi into the pot of boiling salted water. On tonight's menu is chicken and pesto gnocchi with homemade garlic bread.

"She's not her usual bubbly self, and when I ask her how things are going with the wedding, she gives me a 'fine' and then changes the topic."

"I haven't seen her since Wi-ook club the other day where her and Joel got into it."

"What do you mean 'they got into it'?"

"They had a fight about smut."

"Let me guess, he told her it was wrong and immoral and he doesn't know why an educated woman like her reads erotica."

"Pretty much that, and it all started cause Mrs. Winters said, 'Any hole is a goal,' in reference to why choose romances."

"Well, she isn't wrong—"

"Lalalalalalalala," I sing. "I don't want to hear about your holes being goals. I'm your brother and I do NOT need that visual."

"Who said it's my holes that are the goals? My husband has hot—"

"Sabrina McMahon!" I shout incredulously. "If I don't want to hear about your holes, I definitely do not want to hear or think about your husband's ... or anyone's, for that matter."

"You're no fun."

"Please," I scoff. "I'm the life of the party, but getting back to Reindeer, you want me to pop over and check on her?"

"Would you mind?"

Yes, because I cannot be held responsible for my actions around her. "Of course, she's like family."

"Thank you," she says and I can hear the smile in her voice. "You know, I used to dream you two would hook up so she would become my sister-in-law."

"Really? You would have been okay with that?"

"Hell yeah, I would have." She pauses. "Would you have gone after her had you thought I'd be okay with it?"

In a heartbeat. And I mean that. Had I known my sister would have been okay with us as a couple, I would have done things differently that Christmas, but I guess Fate had other plans for her since she's about to marry another man. "I mean, maybe, she is kinda hot."

"Kinda? Please, Ruby Olsen is a fucking knockout. If I batted for the other team, I'd have locked her down years ago. If you ask me, Joel should be thanking his lucky stars she wants to marry his boring, stuck-up, prudish ass."

"Tell me how you really feel."

"I just did."

"Does Ruby know you feel this way?"

"God no, you know I can't tell her exactly how I feel. I value our friendship too much to be honest-honest with her about him, but I, umm, I did question her the other weekend in regard to if she's sure about him."

"And what did she say?"

"Nothing really, but they're getting married next week so I guess deep down she does want to marry him."

"Guess so."

"Alcohol always cheers her up so maybe she just needs to get drunk for a night."

"Alcohol is never a good idea but, then again, no great story starts with water."

Then together we cry out, "Or with a salad." I still remember the first time Sabbi sent me the "no good story starts with a salad" meme. I laughed so hard and now whenever we see one, we send it to each other.

With me confirming to check on Reindeer, she starts talking about the girls and their upcoming Christmas performance, which they are both super excited to perform in. I tell her to take heaps of pics for Uncle Maddox and then a silence falls between us. A few moments later, in the background I hear an almighty crash, followed by my sister hissing, "For fuck's sake." A chuckle escapes me and she growls, literally growls at me, "I gotta go, let me know what you think after you see Ruby."

"Will do. Love you, Sis."

"Love you too, Big Bro."

She hangs up and I get back to finishing up my dinner ... and mentally preparing myself to visit Reindeer with a bottle of tequila, or maybe a salad, 'cause bad decisions don't come from salad.

DING DONG

The sound of the doorbell startles me, and looking at the clock, I see it's nearly seven. I've been sitting here, staring into the fire and nursing a glass of red for the last hour and a half. That in itself is odd. By now, I'd usually be on glass number three. The reason for my reverie, Joel stood me up—again.

This time, it was without a call or text, and on top of that, he's not answering his phone, cell, or landline. All five of my texts have gone unread.

Placing my glass down on the coffee table, I hop up and walk toward the front door. The closer I get, I hope it's Joel. Swinging it open, my face drops when I see it's not him. "Mad, what are you doing here?"

He lifts a bottle of tequila up and smiles, as if that explains everything. Furrowing my brow, I look from him to the bottle and back to him again. "Sab said you've had a busy week so we thought tequila might help."

"Tequila never helps, but she's right, it's been a week so, come on in."

Maddox follows me inside and I tell him to take a seat while

I grab two shot glasses, some lime, and salt. Thankfully, I have limes on hand, but then again, a girl always needs to be prepared for an impromptu tequila night.

Half a bottle of tequila later, my face is fuzzy and my stomach hurts from laughing so hard. Maddox has been telling me countless stories regarding calls he's been on over the years. "I don't know how you do it," I tell him as I pour us another shot each. "Each call is so different."

"Keeps the job interesting, that's for sure."

Handing him his shot, we tap glasses and shoot it back … and like every time, I make a "bleurgh" sound when I'm finished.

"I get that but what about the times when it's bad? How do you cope then?" He nods to the tequila bottle. "I'm serious, Mad, how do you deal with the shitty parts?"

"To be honest, I don't know. I just … deal with it."

"That can't be healthy."

"So far, so good," he tells me. "My friends and family help."

"How so?" Shuffling around, I tuck one leg under me and rest my elbow on the back of the sofa, my cheek on my closed fist and stare over at him.

"If I need to talk, they're there. If I need to cry, they don't judge. They let me get it all out and then they make me laugh."

"Well, now that you're back, just know, I'm here for you too."

"Back at ya, Reindeer." From the look in his eyes, I just know what he's going to say next because he hasn't once broached the topic, and I know he's been speaking with his sister—call it my bestie-sense. Seems the two of them have been talking about me behind my back. "Wanna talk about Joel?"

"Nope," I adamantly state as I shake my head. "Plus, there's nothing to talk about. Everything is fine."

"I call bullshit."

"Well, you're wrong. It's fine. Everything is fine."

"You've said fine eleventy-billion times, therefore you are anything but fine."

"I'm…" But I don't know what to say.

"You're what?" he prods.

Needing liquid courage, I grab his glass and I refill them both … then I shoot both back and I let it all out. "I love Joel, I do, with all my heart, but right now I want to strangle him with tinsel."

"You're threatening violence to the sheriff?"

"I don't literally mean it, plus I know you'd help me cover it up if I ever did accidentally kill someone."

"I would. I'd do anything for you, Reindeer."

His words cause me to smile. Reaching out, I take his hand and squeeze. "Thank you, and I'd do anything for you too." A silence falls between us and it's not awkward, it's actually comforting. He begins to rub the back of my hand and it's oddly intimate. I quickly pull it back because nothing should be intimate with Mad. He's my friend. My best friend's off-limits older brother. "As I was saying, I love him but he's been so absent lately. I get he's busy at work, I am too but he's leaving all the wedding stuff to me and it's supposed to be our day." I laugh. "The other day, he had the gall to say weddings are all about the girl so it doesn't matter if he's there or not."

"He actually said that?" I nod. "Did you kick him in the balls?"

Shaking my head, I laugh. "No, it was over the phone but if he was in front of me, I would have."

"Again, threatening violence to a police officer."

"I'll kick you in the balls in a minute if you keep this up."

"Assaulting an officer is also a criminal offense." Picking up the throw pillow between us, I throw it at him and it hits him in the head. "That's it." He stands up and stares down at me. "You are under arrest for assaulting a police officer."

A laugh escapes me and my hand flies to playfully whack him but from my seated position and him hovering, my hand collides with his dick. He covers his junk, bends forward, and groans.

"Oh my God, Maddox, are you okay?"

"You really assaulted an officer now," he grunts through clenched teeth. It's not funny but another laugh breaks free. He glares at me and it just causes me to laugh harder. Soon, he too is laughing and drops back down to the sofa next to me. He looks over at me, his eyes filled with tears. *Oops*, I lean forward and grab the bottle. "Tequila?" I offer, and we once again start laughing.

Maddox is too drunk to drive home so I offer him the sofa since the spare bedroom has been turned into wedding HQ. Grabbing a pillow and blanket from the hall closet, I walk back into the living area and I stop mid step. Maddox has his back to me and has taken his shirt off. Standing here, I stare at his muscular back and when he spins around, he smiles but he also has a smug look that confirms I've been caught checking him out.

"Here." I hand him the bedding, not looking him in the eye. I'm embarrassed at being caught checking him out. "Do you need anything else?" He shakes his head. "Well, I'll see you in the morning."

"Night, Reindeer," he utters.

"Night, Mad."

Turning around, I walk into my bedroom, close the door, and lean against it. *It's just Maddox*, I tell myself. He's only staying here because we drank too much tequila. It's the right thing to do. After my internal pep talk, I push off the door and head into my bathroom to change into my pajamas and brush my teeth.

Flipping off the light, I pad over to my bed, pull back the covers, and climb in. Burrowing under the blankets, I snuggle in and smile. I needed tonight, I needed a night to just let loose and forget. I'm the most relaxed I've been since my weekend with Sab ... I should have cherished this feeling because soon, I will be anything but relaxed.

twenty-four

MADDOX

THERE'S a banging echoing around the room and there's also one in my head too. Tequila is never a good idea, and it definitely isn't a good idea to do shots with the woman you are secretly crushing on … again. "Ugh," I grunt as I push myself up.

Shuffling over to Ruby's front door, I open it and see Joel standing there. "Morning, Joel," I offer in greeting.

"Where are your clothes?" he asks.

Looking down, I see I'm only in my boxer briefs. I remember going to sleep with clothes on, and I vaguely remember removing them in the middle of the night. Sleeping in denim is uncomfortable, and so is Reindeer's sofa. I was planning on being re-dressed before Reindeer woke up. I guess I achieved that, but now I'm face-to-face with her fiancée … without my pants on. Before I can answer, from behind me, Reindeer screeches, "Joel!"

The sound of her voice vibrates through my head and I wince. The man in question leans around me and his eyes widen. His reaction piques my interest so I glance over my shoulder, and I see Reindeer in nothing but a fluffy bath towel.

"Where are your clothes?" he repeats the same question to her.

"I'm about to have a shower but I wanted to let Maddox know there was a towel in the main bathroom for him."

"But why's he here? In his underwear?"

"We had a few drinks last night and he was in no state to drive, so he slept on the sofa."

"Why not in the spare room?"

"If you'd have been here at all this week, you'd know the spare room and the dining room have been overtaken with wedding prep."

He ignores Reindeer and focuses on me. "But why are you practically naked?"

"Sleeping in jeans is uncomfortable, and when I heard you relentlessly banging, I thought it was urgent and forgot about my pants."

"Can you at least put them on now?"

"Whatever, man."

Leaving him in the doorway, I head back to the sofa and pick up my jeans and shirt and put them on. Once I'm re-dressed, I walk back to the entry where Joel and Reindeer are still standing. The atmosphere is thick with animosity, and it strikes me he never kissed her hello. "I'm gonna head home, Reindeer. Thanks for last night, it was great catching up."

"I had fun too, even if I have a tequila headache this morning."

A chuckle escapes me. "The consequences of a good night. We should do it again when Sab and Eamon get into town for the wedding and Christmas."

"If time prevails, Joel and I would love to."

At the mention of Joel being there too, my smile fades but I quickly school it. I need to get used to Reindeer and Joel being together. I mean, they are getting married. All I will ever be is a chapter of her life.

Stepping over to her, I place a kiss on her cheek and breathe her in. A gasp escapes her when my lips touch her cheek. Looking down at her, I smile. Pulling away, I look to Joel. "Joel," I say with a nod, and without another word I go out to my truck and head home. It's so good having her back and, with all the snow, she handles better than the soccer mom car.

Entering my apartment, I head straight for my bed. I need a few more hours of sleep before work.

Today's shift is dragging.

It's like everyone in town has disappeared, there has not been one call since I got here. I refuse to use the "Q" word—quiet—because uttering that does some voodoo magic and all the crazies come out to play. Not even our illusive doorstep pooper is out and about.

The temperature did drop drastically overnight so people are probably tucked in at home—lucky assholes—drinking hot chocolate with marshmallows while staring into a raging fire and listening to Christmas music. At least I have the Christmas music here.

The clearing of a throat garners my attention and when I look up, I see Joel standing on the other side of the counter. He has a sour look on his face. Standing up, I walk over to where he stands and cross my arms. "Joel, what can I do for you?"

"What's your deal with Ruby?"

"What do you mean, what's my deal?"

"You're always there."

"Huh?" I grunt with confusion. *I'm always where?* 'Cause it feels like at the moment, I'm always at work. What with Ina about to give birth, Stan is splitting his time between home and here. Drew is, well, Drew. But at the moment, he's always out following up leads in relation to our flaming doorstep pooper. He's on the hunt and is determined to find them before Christmas. And Dennis, not sure what's going on with him. Rumors are he and Syd are getting it on, but I don't listen to the gossip. I must say though, seeing him dressed up as Santa on Friday night was the highlight of my year.

"You're always there," he spits at me. "Every time I turn around, you're with Ruby."

"And most of the time you're not," I throw back at him. I know it's a shitty thing to say, but I'm not wrong. I've been back for near on two weeks now, and I think I've seen the guy all of three times.

"I'm busy," he huffs.

"I never said you weren't," I defend myself, and Reindeer. "But from an outsider looking in, you're not doing anything for this wedding and you're not being there for Reindeer. She's doing it all."

"It's her day," he shouts at me.

"Joel, it's your day too. A wedding is the joining of two people. Two." He stares blankly at me. "Look, you seem like a nice guy and you must be, otherwise Reindeer wouldn't be marrying you, but you need to think hard about if this is right for you. Don't get married just for her, that's a recipe for disaster. Get married because she's your first and last thought every day. Because the thought of not having her in your life is unbearable to think about. Joel, if you truly love Reindeer, man the fuck up and be there for her."

He just stands there. No emotion on his face. It's as if my words fell on deaf ears but then, in the blink of an eye, he grows some balls. "You have no idea about my relationship with Ruby. It's between us and us only. It's *our* wedding, Sheriff. I will do what I need when I'm needed, but it's her day. Always has been, always will be. You need to butt out of our life and let us be. Things between us were fine till you arrived." He takes a deep breath and I'm kind of impressed he's finally manning up, but then he spoils it with his next statement. "You know, I'm starting to think that the two of you are having an affair."

"How dare you speak about her like that?" How dare he accuse her of that, who does he think he is? "If you know her as well as you claim to, you know she's not a cheater, and for the record, if she was mine, I wouldn't even have to think about that because she would be my everything and she'd know that."

Luckily for him, the station phone rings because I was about to jump over the counter and belt that thought out of his little head. Reindeer is not a cheater and neither am I.

Answering the call, I take down the details and tell them I'll be there in five. There's been a car accident on the road into town; seems Murray the fucking Mule Deer has caused another incident. A tourist was out for a Sunday drive, they swerved to miss Murray and, in the process, ran into another car coming the other way.

Hanging up, I look up and see Joel is gone. He's a weird one, and I do not see what Reindeer sees in him but it's none of my business, even if he is accusing me of having an affair with his fiancée. Shaking off thoughts of Joel and Reindeer, I grab my hat and head out to the accident to see what damage Murray the Mule Deer has caused.

twenty-five

RUBY

"MADDOX EVANDER WHITWORTH," I shout as I storm into the station. I don't even know if he's here at the moment, but my anger is clouding my judgment and rational thinking right now. Thankfully, when I reach the counter, I see him standing there but when my eyes land on him, my anger intensifies. "What the fuck were you thinking?"

Why am I angry, you ask? Well, I just got off the phone with Joel, surprise-surprise, he can't make it to the meeting with the planner and me tomorrow because he has a late meeting he forgot about, but that's not why I'm pissed. I'm pissed because he told me that yesterday he and Maddox had a fight, about me and him.

"You'll need to be more specific than that, I think about lots of things. For instance, does a straw have one hole or two? How do nudists clean their glasses? Why isn't the plural for ibis ibi?"

Dennis interrupts me, "Is there a synonym for synonym?"

"Ohhh, that's a good one," Maddox says to Dennis.

"There is," I answer. "Equivalent or alternative words."

"Hmmmpf, there you go," Dennis says, nodding. "Okay, then, is the S or C silent in scent?"

Nodding, I purse my lips at his question, but then I shake my head. I'm here for a reason and discussing random facts is not why I'm here. "Focus," I growl at the two of them. "Now answer me, Whitworth."

"What specific thought are you referring to if the above didn't cover it?"

"Joel thinks we're having an affair because you said I'm your everything."

"No, I said *if* you were mine, you'd *be* my everything. Big difference."

"Why would you say that?"

"Because he's being an inconsiderate dick, Reindeer."

"He is not," I snap in Joel's defense.

"Who helped with the thank-yous and cooked dinner for you?"

"You did."

"Who cheered you up with tequila the other night when you were stood up, again?"

"You did."

"Right, and I did those things as your friend. If he's jealous of our friendship, that's on him. Not me and not you."

"But—"

"No, Rubes. He doesn't get to accuse us of anything. If anything, his behavior alludes to *him* cheating. He's cancelling on you constantly. Recently he's stopped texting and calling. Classic cheating behavior."

"But he confronted you about cheating?"

"Maybe to appease his guilt."

"Ohh," I quietly utter and I think about his statement. Looking up, I stare at him, then at Dennis. "Do you think he is?"

"Nahhh," Dennis emphatically states with a shake of his head. "Dude's too straitlaced and square for that."

Looking to Maddox, I wait for his reply. He looks hesitant to answer, especially when he lifts his arm and squeezes the back of his neck. His go-to action when he's anxious. "If you were mine, there's no way I'd cheat on a girl like you, and there's no way you would ever doubt that I might. Look, I don't really know Joel, but you do. What do you think? Deep down you'll know if he is or isn't."

"I … I don't know," I honestly answer and my eyes well with tears over the fact I'm not sure if he would or wouldn't cheat on me. I should be able to answer that with an unequivocal no, but, right now, I'm so confused about everything.

When I marched into the station, I had one thing on my mind, to yell at Maddox for interfering, but now, he's turned it all around. He's got me doubting myself and Joel. What kind of fiancée am I to doubt him like this? To doubt either of us? "I-I-I have to go," I stammer and before anyone can say anything, I race out of the station and head back to the store. However, I detour by the town square and drop down onto a bench. Lowering my head, I stare at the snow-covered ground.

I'm so confused about everything right now, but I mentally slap myself. It's the middle of the workday during what is always a busy week for us, what with it being just before Christmas, and I left Charlene alone after my call with Joel. It was a really shitty thing to do because the place was full of customers. I may be the boss and can do as I please, but that was really unprofessional of me. Pushing myself up, I power walk back to Read Between the Wines.

As soon as I enter, a sense of calm washes over me and I know it will all work itself out, just like it always does in many of the books I stock. My eyes land on a frazzled Charlene and, instantly, I feel bad for leaving her alone.

Jumping behind the counter, I get to work helping the customers waiting for service. For the next few hours, I flit between the book section and the wine bar, going about my day doing what I love, talking about books and wine.

The rest of the day passes by in a blur, and before I know it, Charlene is locking the front door and flicking on the closed sign.

After closing up, I wave goodbye to Charlene, after apologizing for the millionth time for leaving her in the lurch today, and I watch her climb into her boyfriend's car and drive off. She offers me a wave and I wave back. I'm not ready to head home yet, so I dump my things into my car and I take a walk around town.

The sun is starting to set and the sky is a symphony of colors consisting of red, yellow, orange, and even purple. Pulling my coat around me tighter, I shove my hands in my pockets and off I go. Walking around town this time of year is magical. Storefronts are decorated for the annual window contest. Fire hydrants have bows attached to them and there's even speakers that blast Christmas music throughout town, that's a new addition to our holiday decorations. Mayor Sanchez really went all out this year, wanting to capture the exposure after a lifestyle blogger stayed here last year and shared with all her followers the wonders of Evergreen Lake. It's been great for business but I am looking forward to my honeymoon and getting away from the hustle and bustle for two weeks.

As I pass by Rizzo's, I decide to treat myself to pizza for dinner since I have a lovely bottle of red at home. Placing my order, I take a seat to wait, my stomach growls at the amazing scent coming from the kitchen and I know I made a good choice.

Scrolling my phone, my head is down, but I hear a deep voice I'd recognize anywhere. "Is my order ready yet?"

"Not yet, sorry, Sheriff," Leo informs him, just as Delivery

Dan comes in to collect another three orders for delivery. Seems everyone wants pizza tonight but then again, Rizzo's makes the cutest pepperoni tree pizza this time of year. Not sure what it is, but the tree shape makes it taste a million times better than a round pepperoni pizza.

Maddox turns around and his eyes widen when he sees me also sitting here.

"Hi, Maddox," I offer with a wave.

"Ruby," he replies as he takes a seat across from me to wait for his order.

"You called me Ruby."

"Well, it is your name," he snaps.

"You always call me Reindeer and this is the second time today you've used my name."

He nonchalantly shrugs at me, not saying anything else. It seems he's still pissed at me after my earlier outburst. "You don't get to be angry with me, Maddox."

"I'm not angry," he hisses, crossing his arms across his chest in a defensive pissed-off manner.

"Your words and demeanor say otherwise."

"Don't presume to know my ticks."

"Why are you being a jerk?"

"I'm not. I just want my pizza."

"This is more than having to wait for your pizza and you know it."

"I've had a long day. I don't have time for this shit."

Before I can get answers, Leo calls out his name. Maddox stands up, gets his order, and heads out without a goodbye. Him not saying bye hurts more than it should. I thought we were friends, but it seems I know nothing when it comes to the opposite sex right now.

twenty-six

MADDOX

THIS WEEK HAS BEEN SHIT, and I'm turning into the Christmas Grinch.

It all started on Monday when Ruby and I fought about Joel, and it progressively got worse after that. Especially, when I got a call from my sister on Wednesday yelling at me for making her best friend upset. It didn't matter what I said, it was the wrong thing. Apparently, we can think what we think about Joel and Ruby, but we're not actually supposed to tell them what we think. I don't get that girl logic but I promised Sabbi, in the future, I would keep my mouth shut. Then we made arrangements to have dinner with the family at the Powder Room on Friday night and now, here we are.

I'm sitting next to Cass and she's telling Mom, Dad, and me all about how Braydon Jayden—yep, that's this kid's name— got a pet hedgehog, named Mario the Hedgehog, and her mom, who just got massive stink eye across the table from her daughter, is being a "big meanie head" and won't let her have one.

The sound of someone gasping garners my attention and when I look up, I see Reindeer standing beside the hostess. She looks shocked to see me but she quickly schools it when my sister jumps up. The two of them hug like long-lost friends who haven't seen each other in forever and not just a few weeks ago. "I can't believe you're getting married in two days' time."

"I know. It's come up so fast," she tells Sabbi.

She looks gorgeous tonight. She's wearing a stunning black number that highlights her tits and curves. Her hair is dead straight and it hangs over her shoulders.

"You got something on your chin," Eamon says, garnering my attention.

Lifting my hand, I wipe at my chin but there's nothing there. When I look to Eamon, he has a smirk on his face and his gaze flicks from Reindeer to me and back again.

Scowling at him, I shake my head, stand up, and walk over to the bar. I order myself a beer and a glass of red for Reindeer. With our drinks in hand, I walk back to the table and place the glass in front of her. "Thanks," she says with a smile. It's the first time she's smiled at me in over a week, and she's never looked more beautiful.

Taking my seat again, Cass continues to tell me all about Braydon's hedgehog. I listen to her blabber on and on but my gaze and attention is on the woman across from me, who is doing everything she can not to look at me.

Her phone rings and she excuses herself to take it. "Joel, where are you?" she hisses into the phone as she steps away from the table.

"That buttface better not be standing her up," my sister snarls, her eyes locked on her best friend.

"Buttface, really?" I tease my sister as I sip on my beer.

"I'm trying to curb my swears in front of the girls."

"And how's that going?"

"Well, considering Monique called a boy at school a," she

leans across the table and whispers, "'fuckfaced, pin-dicked weasel' not very well at all."

Throwing my head back, I let out a belly laugh but it quickly evaporates when suddenly, Sabbi pushes her chair back and races over to a visibly upset Reindeer; Joel isn't coming.

When Reindeer comes back, the mood around the table is somber. She's throwing back glasses of red wine like they're soda pop. Seems she's drinking her feelings tonight. Sabbi manages to get her to eat something, but she's already on her way to a massive hangover tomorrow.

Mom and Dad take the girls back to the cottage they're sharing with Sabbi and Eamon, and now the adults are going to have some kid-free time. Which, knowing my sister, will involve a quickie in the restroom with her husband.

She and Eamon are couple goals and, one day, I hope to have a love like the two of them … but it won't be with Ruby Olsen because in two days, she's marrying another man.

The girls are in the bathroom together and while we wait for our drinks, Eamon pounces. "You have two days to man up, Maddox, and then you'll have missed your chance."

"I have no idea what you're talking about," I tell him, but that's all I have been able to think about all night long, ever since Joel cancelled on Reindeer, again. Actually, if I'm honest, it's all I've been able to think about since that door swung open when I first got back to town, and Reindeer was standing there.

"You keep telling yourself that, buddy, but for what it's worth, I've been rooting for the two of you for years."

"What?" I ask, shocked at his words.

"Blind Freddie can see you two have the hots for one another."

"She's about to marry another man, not sure she has the hots for me."

"Dude, the way she looks at you is how your sister looks at

me. In all the times I have seen her with Joel, not once have I seen her look at him the way she looks at you."

"What are we talking about?" Sabbi says when she rejoins us.

"Nothing," Eamon and I voice at the same time. She eyes us suspiciously but she doesn't push the subject.

"Where's Ruby?" Eamon asks.

"She's chatting with Mayor Sanchez. He was asking her about some books for Mrs. Sanchez for Christmas." Sabbi laughs. "Even though she's three sheets to the wind, bookstore owner Rubes is present and she's chatting away happily. It's the first time she's been happy since that fuckfaced, pin-dicked weasel—"

"I thought the kid correct term is butthead?" I interrupt her.

"Ohh, he's that too," she growls.

"So he's a butthead, fuckfaced, pin-dicked weasel?"

"Who's a butthead, fuckfaced, pin-dicked weasel?" Reindeer asks as she joins us.

"Ohh, umm, the doorstep pooper."

"But I thought Dennis got him?"

"He did but the guy is still a butthead, fuckfaced, pin-dicked weasel. Who does that?"

"Clearly butthead, fuckfaced, pin-dicked weasels do," Sabbi adds with a chuckle.

"I find it hilarious he did it to Dennis. Of all the houses in town to do it to, you don't do it to a sheriff's deputy."

"Dennis was pissed, that's for sure. I've never seen him so angry before."

"Well, wouldn't you be if someone set a bag of shit on fire on your front steps?" Reindeer throws back at me, her hand on her cocked hip. She's looking at me in a way that's supposed to be menacing but due to her drunkenness, she looks cute.

"Touché," Eamon agrees.

"And don't get me started on Drew. He was just as pissed because Dennis was the one to catch the door stoop pooper. He'd put in so many hours investigating the incidents, and all it took was a kid shitting at the wrong house to be caught."

"Guess that kid will be having a shitty Christmas," Sabbi says, laughing like a hyena at her own joke.

"Okay, giggles, should we get out of here?" he says to his wife.

"I'm not drunk," she states, and I think she's right. I've seen my sister at her worst and, right now, I reckon she'd pass a field sobriety test.

"I have a bottle of tequila at my place?" I offer, not wanting the night to end just yet. Even though Reindeer is still giving me the stink eye, it's nice to hang with her, my sister, and Eamon.

"Yes," Sabbi shouts, fist pumping the air.

Reindeer reluctantly agrees with a nod. We settle the bar tab and head outside toward my truck. I only had a few beers with dinner so I'm good to drive. We're walking over to my truck when Reindeer stops and grunts. Turning to face her, I note her face has paled and she doesn't look well. Before any of us have a chance to ask if she's okay, she vomits in the parking lot. The smell of it sets Sabbi off and the two of them begin to vomit in unison.

Now, Eamon and I are left to deal with two throwing-up women, just as it starts to snow.

We manage to get the spewing duo into the back of my truck, and I threaten both of them with death if either of them throws up in my car. I drop Eamon and Sabbi off first and help him get my now comatose sister inside.

Climbing back in, I look at Reindeer in the back, her head rests against the window and she's staring into space. Putting the truck into gear, I head toward her place. Pulling into her driveway, I glance backward and see during the drive here, she passed out. Her head has dropped forward and cute little snores come from her. Worry slams into me that she may throw up and choke in her sleep, so I make the decision to take her back to my place so I can watch over her. Leaning into the back, I lay her down across the back seat and kiss her on the forehead before I take her back to my place.

twenty-seven

RUBY

"UGH," I groan. "I think I'm dying."

My head is pounding, and my mouth feels like what I'm guessing a dirty ashtray tastes like. Cracking my eyes open, I furrow my brow when I don't recognize the bed or bedroom I'm in. Lifting the blanket, my eyes widen when I see I'm in a tee that's definitely not mine … or Joel's. "Where the fuck am I?" I grunt, flinching at the harshness of my voice.

"You're up." The sound of Maddox's voice startles me, and when I look toward where it came from, my eyes widen when they land on him. He's standing in the doorway to what is obviously his bedroom. He stands there shirtless, with a backward cap on his head and in gray sweatpants.

Gray.

Fucking.

Sweatpants.

Holy book porn, Batman. Never have I seen anything hotter than what is before me right now. Pushing myself upright, I cross my legs and take a calming breath. Lifting my gaze, I look over to Maddox. He's now leaning against the doorframe, his arms are across his chest and his muscular biceps are waving their jazzy "look at me" muscles in my face. "Why am I here?"

"What do you remember?"

Someone asking that is never a good thing, but I think back on last night. "Ummm…" As I think, it all comes crashing back to me and my eyes open wider in shock, disgust, and embarrassment. "Oh my fucking God! I vomited."

"Several times," he confirms. His cheeky tone pisses me off, as does the smarmy look on his face.

"But me vomiting doesn't explain why I'm here."

"You passed out in my car while we were dropping off Sabbi and Eamon. I didn't want to leave you alone in case you vomited in your sleep, where you'd choke and die. So, I brought you here, which was a good thing because at stupid a.m., you woke up and vomited all over yourself and the bathroom."

"Oh my God," I cry again. Falling back to the mattress, I cover my face in embarrassment.

"I cleaned you up and you started to cry—"

"Oh my God, stop. Just, please stop."

Ignoring me, he continues, "Amongst your sobs, you told me you loved me and I'm so pretty." He chuckles and is grinning like a carnival clown right now at my embarrassment.

Sitting up, I glare at him. "This is not funny, Maddox."

"From where I'm standing it is."

"Ugh, I hate you right now, but do me a favor?"

"Anything."

"Put some fucking clothes on."

Pushing off the doorframe, he heads into his closet to grab a shirt. He steps back into the room while pulling it over his head.

"That's not any better," I hiss at him when he looks to me, once again grinning. He grabbed a navy tank that's a little on the small side and does nothing to hide his muscular physique.

"You're cranky when you're hungover, but luckily for you, I have the best cure."

"A time machine so I can go back to the past and not drink so much?"

"Sorry, I don't have access to a Tardis, but I can whip you up a bacon and egg wrap with extra bacon, crispy."

"And coffee?"

"Of course."

"Fine, but can I grab a shower first? I feel all icky."

"Sure." He nods. "Your clothes should be dry soon, I've just popped them into the dryer."

"You didn't have to do that."

"I did, they were covered in vomit."

"Ohhh, well, umm, thank you."

"There are spare towels under the sink and when your clothes are dry, I'll pop them on the bed for you."

"Thanks, Maddox. I appreciate you looking after me."

"It's what friends do when one of them gets shitfaced."

"But are we friends? I was kind of horrible to you the last time we spoke, and last night I was a terse surely bitch."

"We'll always be friends, Reindeer."

We stare at one another, and we let his words hang in the air. Once the uncomfortableness reaches fever pitch, he walks out, closing the door behind him.

Dropping back to the mattress, I stare at the ceiling. This is all Joel's fault, he should have been there last night. Speaking of, my phone begins to ring from the side table.

"Where are you?" he says by way of greeting when I answer. "I'm at your place to get you for the final meeting with the wedding planner before tomorrow."

"Shit," I hiss. "I'm with Sab." The lie falls off my tongue like a hot knife through butter.

"Where are you and I'll come get you guys."

"We'll meet you there," I tell him. "We'll be like ten minutes behind you."

"Fine," he huffs and hangs up.

Dialing Sab's number, I climb out of bed and turn in circles, not sure what to do right now. "Why are you calling me at the asscrack of dawn?" she grunts into the phone. She's as hungover as I was five minutes ago but after that call from Joel, I'm sober now.

"Joel just called to see where I am 'cause we're supposed to be meeting with the planner in half an hour."

"Where are you?"

"I'm at Maddox's in his shirt and I need clothes and for you to come and get me."

"Why are you at Mad's in his shirt?"

"I vomited and he looked after me after we dropped your drunken ass off."

"Aw, that's sweet. Who knew my brother could be so nice? Eamon the f-u-c-k face left me on the sofa, and I woke up to Cassie staring at me asking to get a pet hedgehog."

I can't help but laugh. "Maybe you should just get her one."

"Not you too," she whines.

"Well, the answer seems simple to me."

"Do you want me to pick you up and save your sorry ass?"

"Are you able to drive?"

"No, but Eamon will since he left me on the sofa last night; he owes me big time."

"Can you bring me a change of clothes too? Not sure my little black dress from last night is the correct attire for when you're about to finalize the plans for your wedding."

"But you looked hot in that dress."

"I know, but it's not appropriate."

"Look at you being all responsible. I'll be there in ten."

"Real ten, Sab, not your twenty-minute version of ten minutes."

"Fine, fine," she agrees. "See you soon."

Surprisingly, she arrives exactly ten minutes later, and I quickly change into the jeans and sweater she brought for me, perks of being the same size as your bestie. Then she and Eamon whisk me up the mountain but by the time I arrive, Joel is gone. Apparently, he signed off on everything and left to, surprise-surprise, head back to work.

Sitting in the back of the car, I stare out the window and watch the snowy fields pass by. I'm supposed to be getting married tomorrow, and I'm not even one bit excited.

We stop by the cottage to grab Sab's bag, and then Eamon drops the two of us off at my place, since we'll be getting ready for the wedding here tomorrow. Waving bye to Eamon, we head inside and like the other week, Joel has another surprise for me. A full body massage for two followed by a picnic with wine—ugh—and cheese and deli meats for two.

"He does love me," I mumble as I walk into my bedroom to change for my massage. With this surprise, finally, I'm excited for tomorrow but much like the upcoming storm, my life is about to be thrown into chaos.

twenty-eight

MADDOX

"WHO PISSED IN YOUR BOOTS?" Dennis asks, dropping onto the edge of my desk.

"No one, why?"

"When you first got here, you were Cindy from *The Grinch* excited for Christmas and all that shit. And now you've turned into the Grinch himself."

"I'm not that bad," I snap at my deputy, but he just eyes me.

"Ever since Ruby barged in here on Monday, you've not been you. I know we're a man down with Stan at home with the family, but that hasn't caused us to be busy. Even though it's the silly season, the silliness has been kept to a minimum this year, touch wood." He taps my desk. "Well, except for our flaming pooper, but I solved Drew's case the other night, and I have no doubt that shit—pun intended—will get crazy soon enough. So, I ask you again, what's got you being Mr. Grinch?"

Letting out a sigh, I look to my deputy and begin from the beginning. "I've been in love with Ruby Olsen since the Christmas I took her virginity—"

"How the fuck has *that* been kept a secret in this town?" Shrugging at him, he shakes his head. "I'm gonna go out on a limb here and sound completely fucking girly, but I think she still has feelings for you too."

"But she's marrying another man in less than twenty-four hours"

"And that's messing with your head? Heart? Both?"

"Yep," I reply, letting the 'p' pop. "But I'm not going to stand in the way of her happiness."

"And you're one-hundred-percent sure he's who she wants?"

"A few hours ago, she went up the mountain with my sister to finalize the wedding details with him. Can't get more final than that."

"Well, actually, until that ring is on her finger and each of them say 'I do,' anything can happen."

Nodding, I lean back in my chair and ponder his words. If I *was* one-hundred-percent sure she felt the same way, I'd be over to her place in a heartbeat, but I'm not. I have to let this play out. As much as it pains me, I'll be there to see her marry Joel because, at the end of the day, I want her to be happy ... even if it's with another man.

twenty-nine

RUBY

TODAY IS the day I marry Joel.

Today is the day I get my happily ever after.

My heart is racing. I wish Pop was here to impart some wise words of wisdom before he'd walk me down the aisle, but since he's not, I have Sab telling me a story about Mon and Cass, her nail polish, and the dining table in the cottage where they are staying for the holidays.

Speaking of the girls, Sab has just ducked out to visit them. Apparently, Eamon is having an issue with Cass and she only wants her mom. I told her to go because I need a few minutes to myself. It's been go-go-go since we woke earlier this morning.

Sab and I started our day with a breakfast of ham and cheese croissants, fresh fruit, and mimosas. Then the hair and makeup lady arrived. She worked her magic and then it was time for us to head to the ski resort. I didn't want to wear my dress and trudge through the snow, so we packed our dresses into my car and then we drove up the mountain to the ski resort.

Upon arrival, I duck into the ballroom to check on things and it all looks perfect. The back of the room is floor-to-ceiling windows and it overlooks the mountain. There was a fresh dumping of snow overnight, and it looks magical.

Sab and I make our way to the room where we'll get ready. We have another glass of champagne, 'cause why not, and then it is time to get ready. Sab is dressed in seconds since her dress is simple, but my dress is not as simple. With all the layers of tulle and the corset-style top, it takes Sab almost fifteen minutes to strap me in.

"Thank God Eamon and I took that shibari course last summer," she says as she pulls on my dress. My heads snaps toward her and I chuckle when I see her eyes widen in shock at *that* secret coming out. I make a mental note for us to discuss this at a later date since she was saved by the bell of her daughter needing her.

Taking a deep breath, I walk over to the windows and look out at the snow-covered mountain. Standing here, I watch a skier make his, or her, way down the side of the mountain. Their hips moving side to side as they glide over the snow. I've always been jealous of people who can do that, no matter how many lessons I took, I'm just not a skier … or snowboarder. If there was an Olympics for shit skiing, I'd take the gold in that event with little effort.

The door opens and when I turn around, my mouth drops open in shock because it isn't Sab standing there, it's Joel. "What are you doing here? It's bad luck to see the bride before the ceremony." Then I notice what he's wearing, and I furrow my brows. "Ummm, Joel, why aren't you in your suit? The ceremony starts in fifteen minutes."

He just stands there, staring at me. His hands in his pockets and he rocks back and forth on his heels. The silence in the room is deafening and with each passing moment, a tightness begins to build in my chest … and it's not from Sab tightening my dress too tight. "Joel, what's going on?"

"Ruby, I, ummm, I need to talk to you."

"So start talking," I snap, he flinches at the harshness of my words, but what the fuck? We are due to get married in a few minutes and he's standing here before me all casually and not in his suit.

"I love you, Ruby, but I'm not in love with you."

My eyes widen at his words but I'm too shocked to say anything back to him. My mouth opens and closes and then I finally find my voice. "W-w-w-what do you m-m-mean?" I stammer.

"I don't love you like my dad loves my mom. I can't marry you if I don't love you above everything else. The love I have for you is not husband and wife love, and in good faith, I can't…" He shakes his head but stops mid-sentence.

"You can't what?" I hiss, but I have a good idea of what he's going to say.

"I can't marry you, Ruby."

Blinking several times, I process his words. "And you left it till today, our wedding day, to tell me?" He nods. "You waited until fifteen minutes before the ceremony, while all our family and friends wait for us in a room one floor below where we are right now, to tell me you can't marry me. What the fuck, Joel!"

"I'm sorry," he whispers.

"You're sorry?" I hiss. "You're fucking sorry!" I shout. Anger is coursing through my veins right now. "Is this why you've been distant since the beginning of the month?"

"Partly, yes, bu—"

"Are you seeing someone else?" I interrupt, my stomach rolling at the thought of him being with someone else, and I'm not sure I want to know but at the same time, I do.

"No," he vehemently denies, shaking his head. "There's no one else, Rubes. This is all me, it's not—"

"Are you seriously giving me the 'it's not you, it's me' speech right now?"

"Well, yeah, I am, I guess, but it's true. You're great, Ruby, but we're different people. You're a free spirit who spends her day selling romance novels and wine. I'm a numbers and figures man who spends his day making everything add up, and I've come to realize you and I don't add up."

Standing here, I stare at the man who I thought loved me unconditionally and when he doesn't say anything else, I explode. "The fuck, Joel! You should have told me as soon as you were unsure. I could have saved the heartbreak of having to tell all our friends and family, while I'm in my fucking wedding dress, that my fiancé doesn't want to marry me because in his eyes, we 'don't add up.'" I air quote don't add up but I'm on a roll so I keep going. "I have to tell everyone my fiancé has gotten cold feet and, rather than be honest, he kept it a secret until the last fucking minute." Breathing in deeply, I shake my head. "Get the fuck out, Joel."

"Ruby, I'm sorry. I didn't mean to hurt you."

Shaking my head, I stare at my fiancé, I mean ex-fiancé, and through clenched teeth, I angrily hiss, "Get. The. Fuck. Out!"

"Rubes, I'm sorry," he repeats.

"Get the fuck out," I cry again and, for emphasis, I pick up my bouquet from the table and throw it at his head. The white roses collide with his face and petals rain down around him. Not wanting to look at him anymore, I turn around and stomp into the bathroom, slamming the door behind me.

Leaning against it, I close my eyes and shake my head.

This is un-fucking-believable.

I've been dumped at the altar on my wedding day.

My eyes well with tears and then I start cackling like a witch. My breakdown is interrupted when there's a knock on the door, followed by Sab's voice. "Ummm, Rubes, why is your bouquet on the floor in pieces?"

Taking a deep breath, I turn around and open the door. Opening my mouth to tell her, I freeze when I see her standing there in her bridesmaid dress. Her hair is all fancy in an updo so it shows off the frilly neckline of her dress. She looks like a princess. "Rubes?" she utters my name and that's when water-works start.

Standing in the doorway to the bathroom, I begin to sob and being the friend the she is, without a word, she opens her arms and envelops me in the biggest best friend hug as I break down in her arms.

I'm not sure how long we stand here but finally my sobs stop. Wriggling in her arms, I pull back and stare at my friend. My mouth opens and closes but I don't know how to voice what's just happened because I've come to realize I'm okay with this not going ahead. I'm upset he left it until the last minute and is leaving me to deal with the fallout, but I'm not upset I'm not getting married today.

Reaching up, she wipes under my eyes and her fingers come away black. I must have the biggest raccoon eyes right now, and that causes me to cry again because my makeup was so pretty.

"Why are you crying?" she murmurs as she takes my hand on her. "What's happened?"

"Joel called off the wedding and now I have to tell every-one," I tell her.

From the entrance to the room, a deep voice bellows, "He fucking did what?"

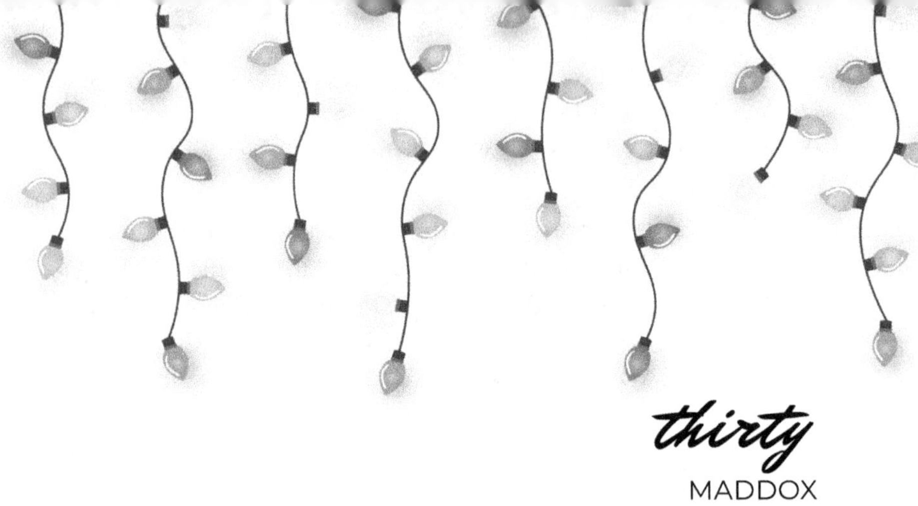

thirty

MADDOX

THE SOUND of my loud voice causes my sister and Reindeer to jump in fright before the both of them turn their heads toward me. My sister has a murderous look on her face, while Reindeer's eyes are red-rimmed and tear marks streak down her face, leaving a trail of black ink in their wake. Even with her face all messy, she's still stunning. And that dress of hers is gorgeous and so her.

"Maddox," Reindeer whimpers. "What are you doing here?"

"I wanted to apologize for, you know what, but it looks like I now need to hide a body after I murder that pin-dicked weasel for doing this to you."

"Don't," she blubbers, while shaking her head. "I just—" She steps around my sister and flops down onto the sofa, the skirt of her dress puffing up and billowing around her.

"Just what?" Sabbi asks, dropping down beside her. She takes her hand in hers and squeezes in that Sabbi way. "What can we do?"

"I ... I just want to get out of here."

Sabbi starts nodding and I can see a plan forming in her

144

mind. "Right, okay, here's what we're going to do." She jumps up and points at me. "You, you're going to get Rubes out of here. I'll go deal with everyone and I'll tell them to all head home an—"

"Tell them to enjoy the reception," Reindeer interrupts her.

"What?" my sister screeches.

"Tell them to enjoy the reception, there's no need to let the food and alcohol go to waste."

"You sure?" my sister questions, confusion on her face. She's thinking what I was thinking, what the hell?

Reindeer nods and a lone tear falls down her cheek. "I'm sure," she softly says, nodding her head and twisting her fingers. She looks devastated and if she didn't need me right now, I'd hunt that asshole down and beat him up. She bats at her cheek, takes a deep breath, and then looks to me with determination. "Let's go."

"Do you wanna get changed?"

She shakes her head. "It'll take too long to undo and I ... I just wanna get out of here."

"O-o-o-o-okay," I stammer just as Sabbi shouts, "You can take my coat."

"Where's your coat?" I ask because it's the middle of winter and there's a storm coming.

"After we got here, Sab took my things down to the car to make it easier at the end of the night for our quick getaway. I was planning on being snuggled up to my husband and using him for warmth, hence my not needing my own coat. Which in hindsight was probably stupid since it'll be dark and there'll be a chill in the air."

Nodding, I process her words and then when my sister hands Reindeer her coat, I shake my head. "Sabbi, she doesn't want to look like a marshmallow," I state. My sister owns this

ugly as fuck, bright-pink fluffy coat that looks like a marshmallow. You can never lose her in a crowd when she wears it, hell,
I'm sure they can see her from the space station.

"I love your marshmallow," Reindeer says to Sabbi, who like
the mature mother she is sticks her tongue out at me. Grabbing
the coat, she helps Reindeer into it and, now Reindeer looks like
one of those toilet roll covers from the seventies due to the puffy
white skirt of her dress and the pink fluffy jacket on top.

"Let's do this," I tell her.

She and Sab hug it out and then I offer her my hand. She
slips hers into mine and with a final wave to my sister, she
walks toward the door. Sab mimics "call me" with her fingers
and I nod my confirmation.

Reindeer and I stealthily make our way down to the parking
garage and to my truck. Helping her into the passenger seat, I
climb into the driver's seat and back out of my spot. "Where
to?" I ask as we start winding our way down the mountain back
to Evergreen Lake.

"Somewhere Joel won't find me," she morosely says.

"I know just the place," I tell her.

She nods and then rests her forehead against the window.
Unlike the last time when she was drunk and ready to pass out,
this time she's upset. As we reach the outskirts of town, she
silently begins to cry again. Her shoulders bob up and down as
she cries. Reaching over, I squeeze her hand, I hate seeing her in
pain like this. The sky above is dark and gloomy. It looks like
we're in for a doozy of a snowstorm, guess the weather is
angry too.

Pulling into my apartment's driveway, I make my way to my
allocated spot and turn the engine off. "Reindeer, we're here."

She lifts her head and looks around. "Your place?"

"Joel won't find you here, he doesn't even know where I
live."

She nods her head and without saying anything, she opens the truck door, climbs out, and walks toward my apartment. Following her, I unlock the front door and step aside, letting her pass. "So, what do you want to do?"

thirty-one

RUBY

"WHAT TIME IS IT?" I ask, shuffling out of Maddox's bedroom. I'm still in my wedding dress and like the last time I woke up here, my head is throbbing and my mouth, once again, feels like a dirty ashtray.

"It's just after eight," he says from the sofa.

"In the morning?"

"Evening."

"I slept all day? Why didn't you wake me?"

"You needed your rest." He hops up and walks into the kitchen and watches me as I pour myself a glass of water. "How much of last night do you remember?"

"Not much," I tell him but going by the state of my head and mouth, I drank way too much. I don't usually drink this much, I might have a glass or two with dinner and that's it but in recent weeks, I've overindulged on several occasions.

"CliffsNotes, you spent the night drinking bottle after bottle of wine while eating cheese. You alternated between crying over Joel and lamenting it was the best thing he could have ever done to you."

"Ohh," I reply. "Sorry about that."

"It's fine, you needed to let it all out and I'm glad I was here for you." He smiles at me and I smile back, but I'm not sure smiling is the right thing to do right now. "How are you feeling now?"

Shrugging, I shuffle into his living area and over to the window. Looking out the glass, there's white for as far as the eye can see. Turning around, I lean against the window. "I seem to have a habit of waking up in your bed hungover, but it's Monday, why are you not at work?"

"The storm that came in was a nasty one. People are snowed in all over the place. Dennis is at the station and has everything under control. He said he'd call if he needed me."

Nodding, I walk over to the fireplace, the warmth seeps into my frozen bones. Looking down at his small tree, I smile as I stare at the smallest Christmas tree I have ever seen, and then my eyes widen. Dropping down to my haunches, I reach through the tulle of my dress and carefully hold one of the ornaments in the palm of my hand.

"It's gorgeous, isn't it?" he says from behind me. "As soon as I saw it, I had to have it. It was like it was calling to me."

Turning my head, I look up at him. "Mad, this matches the one Sab got me."

"What do you mean?"

Carefully placing the ornament back in place, I awkwardly shuffle up into a standing position. I really need to get changed but it's going to take forever to get me out of this thing. It might be gorgeous but it's seriously impractical.

Once upright, I walk over to the counter where I left my bag. Digging in, I grab my phone out. I have several missed called and texts but I ignore them and pull up the photo of my tree. Zooming in, I flip the screen around and shove it into his face. He grabs my hand and pulls it back so he can see the screen.

A gasp escapes him when he sees the ornament's matching twin on my tree. "What? How?"

"Sab gave it to me as a gift. The lady told Sab this ornament would lead me to my one true love." Staring at him, I smile when I realize, *he's* my one true love. "I think that's you," I whisper.

"What?"

"Each time I asked for it to show me my true love, you appeared. At the cottage with Sab, and again at my place a few days later."

Lifting my gaze to his, we stare at one another. Each of us processing what I just said. Reaching out, Mad cups my cheek in his palm and I lean into it. My face fits in his hand perfectly, like they were made to fit.

Staring into his eyes, I whisper, "I think you're my true love, Maddox Whitworth."

"I think you're right, Ruby Olsen."

Like the night of our first kiss, our heads begin to move and he presses his lips to mine. Only one other kiss has ever felt so perfect before, and it was our first kiss when I was nineteen. Pulling apart, he whispers, "Reindeer, we're two halves of one ornament, and I've come to realize Joel doing what he did didn't break your heart because it already belonged to someone else."

He pauses and I whisper, "You."

"Yep, me," he agrees. Tearfully, I nod because he's right. He's so fucking right. "It's always belonged to me, Reindeer, and it has since you were nineteen."

"Just like yours belongs to me."

Before I can say anything else, he slides his hand around the back of my neck and pulls me toward him again. Our lips crash together and with that one touch, with this one kiss, I feel whole. I'm where I'm meant to be. I know I'm with the man from my dream and the one the lady foresaw, a giggle escapes me.

"Do I want to know why you're laughing while kissing me?"

"Because your sister was right. That ornament did lead me to my true love, in a roundabout kind of way."

"Let's not tell her that, her head is already big enough, besides, I've been in love with you since that Christmas we spent together in secret."

"Really?"

"Really, really." Covering his mouth with mine, my tongue slides into his and I give myself, heart and soul, over to him.

"Will you be mine, Reindeer?" he asks against my lips. "I know you just got dumped at the altar but this feels right. We feel right."

Nodding, I swallow the lump forming in my throat. "I'll be yours," I murmur. "I've always been yours, Mad, now kiss me."

Without acknowledging my words, he slams his lips to mine and just like they do in the books I read, as he kisses me, my leg lifts.

My.

Leg.

Lifts.

I smile into the kiss as love and happiness radiate through me and into him.

He slides his hand down my body and drops to his knees. Slipping his hand under the tulle of my dress, he runs his fingertips ever so lightly up my legs, leaving goosebumps in his wake. He rises to his feet and stares into my eyes. I can feel his gaze deep in my soul. He presses his lips to mine, while under my dress he runs his finger over my panty-covered pussy lips. I moan into his mouth and grind myself on his hand. He pushes the soaked material of my panties to the side. Closing my eyes, I hold on to his neck as he thrusts his digit into me and I focus on the sensations firing between my thighs.

With each flick of his wrist, I fall under his spell. In and out he pumps his fingers. Pleasure builds deep within and when I open my eyes, I stare into the chocolate-brown orbs of the man who I have loved for most of my life.

"I'm close," I pant.

"Come for me, Reindeer," he commands and with one final flick of his wrist, I come. My pussy walls contract around his fingers and my juices coat his hand as my orgasm leaks out of me. Pulling his hand free, my skirt drops back down. He lifts his hand to his mouth and licks my release from his fingers.

Leaning forward, I cover his mouth with mine. I can taste myself on his lips, and even though I just came, I could easily come again. Breaking the kiss, I rest my forehead against his. "Wow," I breathlessly pant. "You know, I dreamed about this," I tell him when my breathing returns to normal.

"I've dreamt about this many times over the years too," he tells me.

"No, I mean I dreamed this exact scenario."

"What do you mean?"

"After Sab gave me the Christmas ornament, that night I dreamed about a faceless man in a suit fingering me in my wedding dress."

"I can do more than just finger you but my suit is in the laundry, will you accept a man in sweatpants?"

"Since they are gray and my weakness, you have a deal."

"Excellent, now what else did faceless me do to you?"

"Well, I woke up before we got further but when I did wake up, my fingers were inside me and I was on the cusp."

"You edged yourself?"

"Well, technically yes, but I finished the job I started when I woke up."

"Maybe you should show me what happened after you woke up."

"You'd like that, wouldn't you?"

"Watching you pleasure yourself? Sign me the fuck up." He pauses and swallows. "I want to do it all with you, Reindeer. Unlike last time, there'll be no sneaking around. I want to shout it from the rooftops that you're mine."

"Yours, I like the sound of that."

"So do I, and now that you're mine, Reindeer, I'm never letting you go. I have so many plans for you."

"And what might those plans be, Sheriff Whitworth?" I drag my fingertip down his chest and stare seductively at him.

"Well, for starters, we need to get you out of this wedding dress."

"And then what?"

"And then, we won't be leaving this apartment until I've had my fill of you."

thirty-two

MADDOX

"THEN HAVE AT IT," she purrs, she bites her bottom lip and stares directly at me. I can feel her gaze in my dick and it begins to harden. Well, it's always hard when she's around but with her standing before me with lust-filled eyes, it's harder than steel.

That's one thing I love about Ruby/Reindeer, she's not shy … in anything she does. She may have been a virgin that Christmas, but she was a quick study. She's happy to ask for, or demand, what she wants. "So, you're telling me, once I strip this dress off of you, I can do whatever I want to your delectable body?"

She swallows deeply and nods.

"Sweetheart, I'm gonna need you to verbalize that confirmation."

"Maddox, once you remove my wedding dress from my body, you can do anything you want to me. An-ny-thing."

Beckoning her forward with my finger, she pushes off the counter and prances across the room. Stopping in front of me, I move my finger in a circular motion, she spins around and gives me her back. My eyes drop to the intricate straps crisscrossing over her torso. "Fuck me, how did you get into this?"

"Your sister," she says. "Did you know she and Eamon took a shibari course together?"

"That is not anything I need to know about my sister and her husband. Now, zip it so I can concentrate on getting you out of this contraption."

She glances over her shoulder and seductively murmurs, "Hurry up, Sheriff. I've been a bad girl, and I need punishing."

My dick thickens in my sweatpants at the thought of seeing my handprint on her ass. "We have two options, I can painstakingly and slowly undo the dress, or I can grab a pair of scissors and cut you out."

She spins around, rests her hands on her hips, and glares at me, "You are not cutting this dress off of me, Maddox. You will show it the care and love that a dress of this caliber deserves."

Raising my hands in surrender, I nod. "Okay. Okay, no scissors."

"Thank you."

She spins back around and ever so slowly I undo her dress. The lower I go, the looser it becomes and then finally, it free-falls down her body, leaving her in her panties and a sexy as hell strapless bra. She spins around to face me and my gaze roams over her body, paying close attention to her perky tits. "That was hands down the best Christmas present I have ever unwrapped."

"There's still a few layers left to unwrap," she softly whispers and before I get a chance to reply, she reaches behind her back and unclasps her bra. It falls to the floor baring her tits to me. Hooking her fingers in her panties, she shimmies them over her hips and down her legs. She steps out of them and her dress, leaving her naked as the day she was born.

She steals over to me and rests her hands on my chest.

"Fuck, Reindeer, you're gorgeous with clothes on, but naked, you're exquisite."

"Thank you, Mad, but we seem to have a problem."

"And what's that?"

"You have far too many clothes on for my liking and as much as I love you in gray sweatpants, I wanna see the goods."

"So you want to objectify my body?" She nods and, once again, bites her bottom lip. "Well, it is the season of giving, and I vow to give you anything you want."

"Well, hurry up because I want you naked."

thirty-three

RUBY

I'VE no clue where all this dirty talk is coming from, but I kinda like this sexy vixen version of me. Standing naked before a fully clothed Maddox is thrilling. I'm eager for him to get naked too but he's just standing there, staring. His gaze is locked on my bare chest and he licks his lips.

"Focus," I growl. "Once you're naked, you can ogle, play with, and suck them all you want."

"It's hard to focus when your tits are staring at me all pointy and hard and perfect."

My cheeks darken, and I lower my head in embarrassment, here I am as naked as the day I was born and the boy, no man, I've lusted over since I was a teenager is talking about my tits as if we're discussing the weather. Sure, he's seen and played with them before, but this time it's different. There's no going back or hiding after this.

"There's no need to be all shy, Reindeer. I know you're a dirty minx, and I plan on devouring every inch of your body."

His words spark something inside of me, I rest my hand on my hip and cock it to the side. Eyeing him, I raise my eyebrows.

"Less talking, Whitworth. More stripping." Lowering my voice, I huskily add, "Then the devouring can begin."

He grabs the opening of his shirt behind his neck and does that sexy one-handed thing and effortlessly lifts it over his head. He drops it to the floor and then, like me a few moments ago, he hooks his fingers into the edge of his sweats and, in one fell swoop, removes them and his briefs. He stands back up straight and now it's my turn to ogle him.

My eyes widen when they land between his thighs. "You ... you pierced your dick?"

"Mmmhmpf," he replies with a nod.

"How did I not see that the other day?"

"So you did peek when we skinny-dipped the other day?"

"Hell yes, I did. I remembered what your body was like but I wanted an updated picture for my memory."

"And now you can have all the pictures your little heart desires."

"Right now, my little heart wants a closer look at this piercing of yours."

"By all means," he says, "but let's take this to the bedroom. I want you to be comfortable when our private parts get reacquainted." He offers me his hand, and when I place mine in his, he pulls me into his body. He wraps his arms around my back and slams his lips to mine.

In the middle of his living room, naked, we make out.

His hands slide down my body and under my ass. Tapping my ass cheeks, I jump and he lifts me up. My arms and legs wrap around him and with our lips fused and me holding on to him like a spider monkey, he walks us into his bedroom.

Placing me on my feet at the end of the bed, I shock him when I grab his upper arms, turn him around, and push him down to the mattress. Dropping to my knees before him, I focus my gaze on his dick. My mouth waters as I trace my finger over the pierced head. The tip leaks precum and I want a taste.

Leaning forward, I stick my tongue out and sweep it over the tip, collecting the liquid. He hisses at the connection and with my eyes locked on his, I lick down and up his shaft before taking it into my mouth, sucking.

"Fuck, Reindeer, your mouth…"

His dick pops out. "My mouth what?" I ask him.

"It's as perfect as you are," he utters.

An idea forms and suddenly, it's all I can think about. I read about this in a hockey book I love and I've always wanted to try it. Taking the chance, I go for it. Leaning forward, I push my breasts together, encasing his cock between my tits. With his cock trapped, I move back and forth. His dick sliding up and down between my mounds. Pushing the head all the way through, I lean down and suckle on the tip.

The metal from the bar in his cock scrapes over the skin of my breasts and the sensation is phenomenal, especially when I grab his dick and circle the pierced head over my nipple before sandwiching it back between my tits.

"I need to fuck you," he grunts.

Nodding my head, I let go of my tits and climb onto the bed next to him. Crawling up the mattress, I reach the pillows, turn, and flop down onto my back. Like a lion stalking his prey, Maddox slowly stalks his way up my body, nipping and sucking along the way before cocooning my body with his. He stares down at me, and I see nothing but lust in his eyes.

"Please fuck me now, Maddox."

thirty-four
MADDOX

"PLEASE FUCK ME NOW, MADDOX."

Best five words she has ever uttered, but I can't quite believe this is about to happen. I've imagined this scenario many times over the years, and I still can't believe it's happening. I mean, technically, right now, she should be on her honeymoon. But instead, she's trapped here with me in my apartment while we ride out the snowstorm that hit, and she hides from everyone after being dumped at the altar.

Is it wrong to want to thank Joel right now for being a complete dickstain and walking away? And then there's Mother Nature, I want to bow down to you for this storm, trapping us here because this is exactly what she and I need.

The way she's looking at me right now is straight out of my memory. So many times, over the years, I dreamed of us getting back together, not that we were together-together, but you know what I mean. I can unequivocally say, this is better than all my dreams and I'm positive it will be as amazing as I remember, if not better.

Not wanting to waste another moment, I lean down and press my lips to hers. She drapes her arms over my shoulders and pulls me closer. Our bodies fit together as if they were cast from the same mold. She grinds herself on my cock, which is harder than it's ever been before. The tip is leaking like a geyser, and I cannot wait to sink myself balls deep inside of her.

Reaching into my bedside table, I grab a condom and sit back on my haunches. With my eyes locked on hers, I tear the foil packet open with my teeth and roll it down my shaft. She spreads her legs open, inviting me in. Gripping the base of my shaft, I line myself up with her entrance and gently push inside.

Inch by inch, my cock slides into her.

It's heaven.

Both of us moan as our bodies become one.

Back and forth we rock as our bodies become reacquainted with one another.

She pulls me down and covers my mouth with hers. She thrusts her tongue into my mouth and it falls in sync with what's happening down below.

My balls begin to tingle, but I refuse to come before her. A man should never come before a woman and, really, she should be one orgasm ahead. *Next time*, I think to myself.

Hooking my arm under her right leg, I sit back and thrust in deeper. "Oh my God, you're piercing is the best thing ever. Fuck, Mad," she groans. Her voice deep, husky, and so fucking sexy.

Slipping my hand between us, I circle the pad of my finger over her clit. Her eyes roll back in her head, she cups her breasts in her hands, and she bites her lip.

"I'm ... I'm ..." She whimpers, unable to finish her sentence as her orgasm builds.

"Come for me, Reindeer," I command and at the sound of my voice, her walls clench me tighter and she explodes. Closing her eyes, she lets out a guttural groan as her body stiffens. Her pussy hugs my cock as she comes and comes and comes.

Opening her eyes, she gazes up at me completely sated. She

realizes I've yet to come and she does this pussy clench around my dick and it sets me off. My body spasms and I come. Spurt after spurt fills the condom, I don't think this much cum has ever come out of me before.

Rolling off of her, I flop down onto the mattress next to her, I lie here, huffing and puffing. When my breathing returns to normal, I sit up and pull off the condom. Knotting it, I drop it to the carpet and lie back down. Reindeer rolls onto her side and throws her leg over me. Slipping my arm under her, she snuggles closer to me.

Absentmindedly, I begin to rub my fingers up and down her arm. Closing my eyes, I let out a contented sigh and smile to myself.

"What was that for?" she asks, lifting her head up.

Opening my eyes, I stare over at her. Her cheeks are flushed, her hair's a mess, but to me, she's never looks so beautiful. "What was what for?"

"That sigh."

"It was a sigh of contentment. I can't remember the last time I was this relaxed. Everything feels..."

"Right," she answers for me. And seeing her smiling so brightly, I know she means it, but then she furrows her brow. "But, umm, what does this mean?"

"What do you want it to mean?"

I hold my breath as I wait for her to answer. She's been through a lot in the last few days, and I don't want to add to those stresses, but at the same time, I don't want to let her go. I know what it's like not having her in my life and now that I've had her again, I don't want to let her go ... ever.

"I want you, but at the same time, I feel like a shitty human for feeling like this. A few days ago, I was supposed to be marrying another man and now I'm with you. Doesn't that make me a ho?"

My head begins to shake from side to side. "You are far from a ho, Reindeer. Sexual deviant, yes, but then again, so am I. So, really, I can't judge you. Your fiancé, well ex-fiancé, left you at the altar. He. Left. You. Yes, deep down it wasn't what you wanted either because your heart belonged to someone else—"

"Modest much?" she interrupts.

"It's not modest when it's the truth and, Reindeer, we were meant to be. Even the ornaments agree with Fate's plan."

"Can I just say, Fate is a bitch because her plan sucked. We missed out on so much time together."

"But we got here in the end. We just had to each go on a separate adventure before we came onto the same path again."

"Who knew you were so poetic?"

"You know what else I am?"

She rests her arms on my chest and leans her chin on top of her hands. "What are you?"

"Hopelessly in love with you." Her eyes widen at my declaration, but I don't want to hold back what I'm feeling. I've hidden how I felt for too long now.

"Say that again," she murmurs.

"I love you, Reindeer. I've been in love with you since—"

She pushes herself up and presses her lips to mine and then, against my lips she mumbles, "I love you too, Maddox. I have since I was a teenager."

Threading my fingers into her hair, I devour her mouth with mine. Rolling on top of me, she sits up and shuffles back. Gripping my cock, she begins to stroke. "I'm on the pill," she whispers, "I want to feel you—all of you."

"Are you sure?"

She nods and I nod too. I've never not used a condom before, I was waiting for the one and, we all know, she's always been the one.

Lifting herself up, she shimmies forward and sinks herself

down on me. It feels so different with a thin rubber layer between us. I can feel every part of her and that sensation intensifies when she begins to ride me.

Reaching up, I cover her tits with my hands and I massage them. Her head drops back and she continues to slide up and down my shaft.

With a strength I didn't know I had, I sit up and slide my arms around her back, my dick stays nestled inside her. She wraps her arms around my lower back, and with our eyes locked on one another, we rock back and forth. Lowering my head, I take a nipple into my mouth and suck. Gently biting down on the taut peak, I feel her walls tighten around my shaft. I'm not going to last long without the barrier of the condom.

There are no words to describe the feeling of fucking her bare.

Thankfully, her orgasm comes out of nowhere and she comes seconds before I do. Together we ride out our release before falling back to the mattress, her still on top of me. Holding on to her tighter, I kiss her hair and thank my lucky stars for getting a second chance with the most amazing woman in the world. I make a silent vow, now that she's mine, I'm never letting her go.

thirty-five

RUBY

LYING HERE in Maddox's arms is like a dream come true, and as if he's in my head, he mumbles, "I'm never letting you go."

I chuckle against his chest and lift my head to stare at him. "Well, you might want to because I need to pee."

"Fine," he huffs and reluctantly he lets me go. Rolling off of him, I climb out of bed. "You better come back," he whines like a petulant child.

Looking over my shoulder at him lying there with sex hair, I grin down at him. "There's nowhere else I want to be, Mad. I'll be right back."

Skipping across his room, I head into the en suite, closing the door behind me. We aren't at the peeing with the door open stage of our relationship yet, and that should have been a red flag with Joel. I was never allowed in the bathroom when he was in there. We couldn't even brush our teeth together. Speaking of teeth, I can't remember the last time I brushed mine.

After using the toilet, I wash my hands and then I grab Maddox's toothbrush, squeeze out some toothpaste, and brush

165

my teeth with it. This is another no-no, according to Joel. He was happy to eat my vagina but sharing a toothbrush was unacceptable.

I'm rinsing my mouth when my phone begins to ring, I smile when I hear the tone, it's Sab. I haven't spoken to her since shit hit the fan with Joel and then Mad whisked me away. We've texted a few times but I haven't actually spoke with her.

"Hey, hey, Sis," I hear Maddox say through the door as I wipe my mouth on the hand towel. My hand is on the door to step out when I hear Sab screech and then it's followed by, "Ooh my God, you two totally fucked."

My eyes widen and I wrench the door open, my eyes are as wide as saucers. Walking over to the bed, I snatch the phone out of Mad's hands and turn the screen to me. "My eyes," Sab cries, covering her eyes. I look down and realize, I'm naked ... and there are love bites on my boobs.

"Please," I scoff at the screen. "We went skinny-dipping the other day."

"That's different, now cover the girls up."

"Fine," I tell her as I walk back into the bathroom and pop my phone on the counter. "Now, while I pull on a shirt, tell me why seeing my tits while skinny-dipping is okay but now isn't?"

"Because now you have sex tits."

"Sex tits?" I repeat.

"Yep, sex tits ... and sex tits from my brother. What the fuck, Rubes?"

Pulling one of Maddox's shirts over my head, I pick up my phone, and walk back into his room. He's sitting on the edge of the bed and he's pulled on his boxers but he's still shirtless, I take a moment to ogle him. "Focus," Sab shouts and I can't help but laugh.

Taking a seat on the bed next to Maddox, I take a deep breath. "So, ummm, there's something we need to tell you."

"No fucking shit. How did this happen? When did this happen? How—"

Maddox grabs the phone from me. "My penis entered her vagina—"

"Lalalalalalallala," she sings. "I don't mean that, you dick-hole. I know how it works, I have two kids ... and I'm married. What I meant was how did this"—she flicks her finger between Mad and me—"happen?"

He looks over at me and with his eyes locked on mine, he tells his sister, "I've been in love with her since she was nine-teen and we snuck around one Christmas."

Another screech echoes through the speaker. "What the fuck?" Then she falls silent. Dropping my gaze, I look at the screen to check if we've been disconnected, but Sab is sitting there speechless, her mouth wide open.

"I think we broke her," I tell Maddox, he looks over at me and gives me that sexy grin of his.

"I think we may have." He looks back to the screen. "You good, Sis?"

"I'm ... processing." Then her eyes widen. "Dear brother of mine, are you telling me the one who got away was my best friend?" He nods. "And that one Christmas, many moons ago, you two secretly bumped uglies and no one knew?" We both nod this time. "And you!" She turns her attention to me. "You kept from me the fact you slept with my brother?" It's my turn to nod. "And now, what, you two are a couple?"

"We are," I confirm. "Is that okay with you?" I hesitantly ask, I'm not sure how I'll react if she's not happy about this.

"Is that okay with me?" Again, Mad and I both nod. "It's more than okay, it means that finally we will be sisters, and you're with the one you were always meant to be with."

"You're not angry?"

She shakes her head, grinning like the cat who got the

canary. "I'm over the fucking moon you two are together, but I'm pissed you both kept secrets from me for the past however many years."

"We feel bad about that, but in all honesty, it was just that time at Christmas you didn't know about. You've known of my crush on your older brother since even before I did."

"Yes, I did call it," she cheekily informs us. "But no specific peen or sex talk. I don't need to hear that about my brother."

"So you don't want to know...." But the rest of that is cut off when Maddox slams his hand over my mouth.

"No penis and/or sex deets," she growls.

At the same time he whispers so only I can here, "I'll give you all the penis you need as soon as we get off the phone." He nips my earlobe and the bite heads straight between my thighs.

"And on that note, I'm gonna go. Hopefully this storm passes before Christmas. I wanna hang out in person with the hottest new couple in Evergreen Lake."

"It's not looking good, Sis. Dennis said it's pretty bad out there and even if it does clear, I'll have to work."

"But I don't," I voice.

"YAY," Sab singsongs. "And on that note, I'm going to let you two lovebirds go, and remember, if it's not on, it's not on." My eyes widen and I remember he and I going bare just before. Not using protection is so much more intimate. More intense ... and suddenly I can't wait to do it again, but a bucket of cold water is splashed on me when Sab screeches, "Oh my God, you dirty slut, you." She cackles and slaps her thigh. "Bet I'll be an aunty before the new year."

Shaking my head, I can't help but grin at my best friend. Only she would go there. Mad and I have only been together for less than a day and she already has me barefoot and pregnant. Don't get me wrong, one day I would like to have Maddox's babies, but let's give it time before we get to that part. For now, I want to enjoy him, and just him.

"Bye, Sis," Maddox calls out, pressing the red hang-up button on the screen. He turns to me and he has a look of hunger on his face. "I'm going to feed you—"

"I'm down for that." I waggle my eyebrows at him.

"Food, I will feed you food."

"Ohhh," I dejectedly pout.

"But after, I'm going to have you for dessert, and then I'm going to fuck you in every conceivable position before we collapse."

"Unless you have lube, you aren't getting near my ass."

"Spoilsport," he whines.

"Not my problem you aren't prepared."

"Well, I wasn't expecting on having naked company over the holidays."

"Touché," I agree with a nod. "Now feed me so you can then feed me with your cock."

And feed me he does. Maddox whips up chicken parmesan, which was delicious, and then he did exactly as he promised. He had me for dessert ... and then he fucked me into a coma.

thirty-six

MADDOX

WAKING up with Reindeer naked in my arms is better than I remember, probably because that Christmas we snuck around I only got to wake up with her once. That was ruined when Dad came into my room at stupid a.m. to see if I wanted to go ice-fishing with him—FYI, I did NOT want to go ice-fishing with him—but thankfully, he didn't notice Reindeer, but at the same time, how did he not notice the naked goddess beside me?

"Morning, Reindeer," I utter when I see her looking up at me.

"Morning, Mad. Sleep well?"

"Like the dead. Some sex fiend kept me up all night long."

"Ha, the same thing happened to me too." She rolls to her side to grab her phone off the bedside table. Pulling her into me, I snuggle into her from behind. My morning wood digs into her ass. I wriggle my hips, trying to slip a quickie in before we start our day, but Reindeer quickly pulls away and rolls over to face me. "I will say it again, and I will keep saying it. No lube, no ass."

"One of these days, I'm gonna shock you and I'll have lube."

"It won't be a shock because I can't wait to feel your pierced cock in my ass."

"Really?"

"Really-really. Now, I'm going to have a shower and then we should look at maybe venturing outside today."

"Ugh, do we have to people? Can't we just stay here naked forever?"

She laughs and shakes her head. "You'd soon get sick of seeing just me naked."

"Never. A thousand years seeing you naked will never be enough."

"You say the sweetest things to me. Now, up. We have shit to do ... plus, it's Christmas Eve."

She climbs out of bed and heads into the en suite. A few moments later, the sound of the shower echoes into my room. She pops her head around the doorframe. "You coming? I might need help washing my back."

Seeing her naked AND wet, yes fucking please.

Quicker than the Flash, I jump out of bed and join her in the shower. We get each other dirty, again, before we wash ourselves clean and hop out.

Since Reindeer only has her wedding dress as an outfit option, I loan her a pair of sweatpants and a shirt. We agree to head to her place for some clothes after we eat.

While I finished getting dressed, she heads into the kitchen to start on breakfast. Before joining her, I quickly call Dennis to check on things. This storm got wild overnight and I want to be sure he's coping. He told me to stay with Reindeer when I spoke to him yesterday, but he shouldn't be at the station alone during a storm, or in the lead-up to Christmas.

"Hey, Sheriff," Dennis says when he answers.

"How you doing? Things all good?"

"All good on the home front, nothing I can't handle. Been out plowing."

"Is that code for something?"

"Ohh, the Sheriff's got jokes."

"You know it."

"But seriously, everything is fine here. Nothing I can't handle."

"That's good to hear, umm, how are things on the Sydney front?" I'm met with silence and that speaks volumes. "You want me to come in?" And that question is coming from Maddox his friend and not Maddox the sheriff.

"No, I've got this. How's Ruby holding up?"

At the mention of Reindeer, a smile forms on my face. "We're good."

"We're?" he repeats. "You finally make your move?"

"Fuck off, asshole. You're as bad as the G-team, but if you must know, we're good. She's good. I'm good. It's all good."

"That's a lot of good." He chuckles. "But seriously, I'm happy for you both. Who knew getting stood up at the altar would have a happy outcome?"

He's not wrong there. When I heard what that pindick weasel did, I was pissed off, but the silver lining of that shitshow: Reindeer and I finally got our chance.

"Fate has a way of working her magic in a roundabout weird and wonderful way."

"Just don't fuck it up," then he softly says, "like I did."

I'm not sure what to say to that since I don't exactly know what he did. "Okay, well, if you need anything just holler and I'll be there." Again, I mean personally and not professionally, even though I'd be there for that too.

"Same goes for you, Mad, and if I haven't said it already, I'm glad you're the new sheriff. The town is in good hands."

We say our goodbyes, and I hang up. Walking out of my

bedroom, I stop and watch Reindeer. She's at the stove, dancing away while bacon fries in the pan. Dean Martin is singing *her* song "Rudolph The Red-Nosed Reindeer" and I start humming along.

Reindeer looks over her shoulder at me and winks. Turning her attention back to the stove, she continues to wiggle her butt and sing while I make my way over to her. Resting my hands on her hips, I begin to sway along with her and sing *my* version of the song. "Ruby the red-nosed reindeer, has a very, very sexy butt. Maddox would like to fuck that sexy, sexy butt."

Reindeer giggles and looks over her shoulder at me. "That last line doesn't rhyme."

"I don't need it to rhyme to talk about fucking your butt." She shakes her head and turns back to the stove. Sliding my hands around her hips, I slide them up and cup her boobs in my hands, grinding myself on her ass. "I very much want to fuck your ass, Reindeer."

"And I very much would love that too but..."

"But what?" I ask since she drifted off.

"We've discussed this plenty of times. You don't have any lube, and there is no way that pierced anaconda is getting anywhere near my ass without proper lubrication."

"Makes mental note to add lube to the shopping list."

"You do that," she states matter-of-factly.

Switching off the burner, she shoves me out of the way with her ass and pops the omelette pan under the broiler. The she spins around and drapes her arms over my shoulders and walks me back to the other side of the kitchen. "After breakfast, I need to go home and change and then get to the shop—"

"But you're on leave."

"Not my shop," she refutes. "I meant Hanson's, but I probably should go and check on Read Between the Wines."

"We can do that, but what do you need at Hanson's?"

"Apart from more food, we need to get some lube so you stop droning on about my ass."

"Lube or no lube, I will always obsess over your ass, have you seen it?"

"Only in the mirror," she says with a shrug.

"Well, as someone who has seen it up close and felt it…" I slide my hands down her back and squeeze said ass. "It's delectable, Reindeer, and I cannot wait to fuck it."

"I'm starting to think you only want me for my ass."

"I want you for more than just that but your ass, definitely a bonus."

She nods and from the look on her face, I can see her brain is ticking away. "Do you have coconut oil?"

"I think so." She eyes me in a "well, get it for me" kind of way.

Pulling away from her, I walk over to the pantry and have a look and way in the back—pun intended—I find an almost full jar. Grabbing it, I spin around and hold it up. "What do you want this for? I don't think I've used it with an omelette before." It seems like an odd combination but she seems happy we have some.

"It's not for breakfast." She walks over to the broiler and flicks it off.

"Then why do you want this?" She walks toward me and rests her hands on the counter beside me. She eyes the jar in my hand, not uttering a word, then she looks back to me. "What …" But the question dies on my lips when she drops my sweats, leans on her hands, and thrusts her ass out, wriggling it. She stares at the jar again and, finally, it clicks in my brain.

"Fuck, I love you," I tell her as I begin to remove the lid. Dropping it to the countertop, it clatters and circles around and around before coming to a stop. Digging my fingers into the jar,

I pull them out and hold up the blob of coconut oil. Stepping behind her, I slap her bare ass cheek. "Spread 'em," I command.

She complies and I slide my oil-covered fingers into her crack. A moan slips free just as she turns her head toward me before I cover her mouth with mine. I push my tongue into hers as I work my fingers into her ass.

"Please," she begs, and who am I to deny her.

Dropping my pants, I oil up my dick that has been rock-hard ever since I realized what she wanted the oil for. Stepping behind her, she leans down onto the countertop and pushes her ass out. Gripping her hips, I slide my dick between her cheeks. Lining my shaft up to her oily puckered hole, I gently ease the tip in. She hisses and I stop. "You okay?"

She nods.

"Should I keep going?"

Again she nods.

Pushing in farther, her hiss turns into a moan once my cock is fully in her ass. Holding on to her sides, I start to move my hips back and forth. She lets out a pleasurable whimper and it's music to my ears. Pulling out, I push back in, and soon, I find a rhythm that has her inner porn star coming out.

"Your pierced dick feels amazing in my ass," she mewls as I continue to thrust into her tight hole. Her ass hugs my cock and I'm close to exploding but I want her to enjoy this for longer than two point five seconds. Sliding my arm around her, I massage her clit before I insert a finger into her pussy.

"Yes," she pants as I shove a second finger into her, curving them around to hit her magic button. An indescribable sounds slips through her lips and I feel her body beneath me tense up. She lets out an ear-piercing screech, mumbles a husky, "Fuck, I'm coming," and her release drips down my hand. With her muscles clenching tightly on both my fingers and my cock. I too explode, spilling my seed in her ass, squeezing her hips as her ass sucks every last drop out of me.

She collapses onto the countertop, breathlessly panting. I stand behind her, panting like I just ran a marathon, with my dick still lodged in her ass. She turns her head and looks at me over her shoulder, she looks sleepy yet sated. "How was that?"

"I have no words," she tells me.

"That good, huh?" She nods. "Fuck, I love you."

"I love you too," she replies. "But do you think you can let me get up? When you're not in the throes of passion, this position is not very comfortable on the hip bones."

"Shit, sorry."

Pulling out of her, I help her up and then I lift her into my arms and walk her back into my bedroom and through to the shower. Dropping her to her feet, she reaches in and turns the water on. Once it's to temperature, she steps under the spray. Standing here, I watch the water cascade down her body. Crossing my arms, I lean against the tiled wall and admire her as she cleans herself up.

That was the sexiest thing I have ever seen or been a part of, and I can't fucking wait to do it again. If I thought I was obsessed with her ass before, now it's next level.

Reindeer lifts her gaze and stares at me, I see nothing but love and admiration reflecting back at me, it's exactly how I feel about Reindeer.

My smile widens when I realize, all my Christmas wishes have come true and it's only Christmas Eve. I already have the most perfect gift ever, Reindeer, and her love.

thirty-seven

RUBY

SUNLIGHT FILTERS in through the gap of the blind and I smile, Mad is behind me and we're spooning. His hand is cupping my boob, and from behind me I can feel his morning wood digging into my lower back. Waking up like this is fast becoming my favorite way to wake up.

Wriggling my butt against his dick, he moans and begins to push himself against me. A smile appears on my face and I can't help but wriggle and push myself closer to him. His shaft slips between my bare crack, but I hiss and wince from the contact. My ass is a little tender this morning. After discovering an alternate use for his coconut oil, Maddox and I have become addicted to anal. The jar is nearly empty but when you're snowed in, what else are you to do?

"Merry Christmas, Reindeer," Maddox whispers into my ear from behind.

Rolling over, I stare into his brown orbs and reach up to cup his cheek. "Merry Christmas, Mad," I croak, my voice husky and sleep filled.

Like two magnets, our heads move together and we kiss

each other good morning. It starts getting hot and heavy but my vagina, and ass, need a break so I reluctantly pull back. Before I can open my mouth to tell him, he presses his finger to my lips, shushing me. "How about I run you a bath and while you're soaking, I'll whip up breakfast before we try and make our way over to Sabbi's for Christmas lunch with the family?"

"You are too good to me, Maddox Whitworth."

"Only the best for my girl." My cheeks heat at his words. "Why are you blushing?"

"You called me 'your girl' and I kinda like that."

"You're blushing over that, when I've fucked your ass and licked my cum from your pussy, those actions are cause for blushing."

"What can I say, I'm a complicated girl."

"No." He shakes his head. "You're my girl and now that you are mine, I'm never letting you go ... especially, now I've had your ass."

"So it's all about my ass, huh?"

"You know what I mean."

"I do, and for the record, you're my man and I love you so very much."

"I love you too." He places a quick kiss on the tip of my nose, it's nice seeing him relaxed and bashful.

"You said something to me about a bath?"

All he says is, "I did." Then he's up and out of the bed, heading into the en suite to run me a bath to soothe my aching ass and vagina.

He returns a few moments later and rips the blanket off of me, causing me to screech at the sudden chill in the air.

"Why did you do that?" I scowl at him.

"'Cause your bath is ready."

"You could have just said that instead of, you know." I drop my gaze to the blankets now at the end of the bed.

"I could have done that but then I wouldn't be able to gaze at your sexy as sin body or do this." He bends down and sucks on my nipple, my traitorous body zings to life and I moan.

"Mad, no, I can't," I beg. My nipple pops out of his mouth and he stares intently at me.

"I know but it's your tits, I couldn't not."

"You are a fiend, now let me get my bath so I can soak my sore body."

"We need to work on your stamina," he teases.

"Excuse me, I think I'm allowed to be exhausted after fucking nonstop for three days."

"Amateur," he throws at me with a wink. Offering me his hand, he helps me out of bed and guides me into the bathroom. Holding his hand, he assists me as I climb into the tub.

A moan slips out as I submerge myself in the hot steaming water. Leaning back, I close my eyes and a smile appears on my face. Even though I ache, I'm happy, stupidly happy.

Standing on the veranda of the cottage, I knock and wait for it to open. It's unbelievably cold this morning, but seeing so much white fluffy snow on Christmas Day is magical. Maddox has his arm around me, keeping me warm, but even if we were in hell and sweating, there's nowhere else I would rather be.

"Merry Christmas," Sab singsongs when she swings the door open. She rented the same one we stayed in the other weekend and it really is a perfect lakefront cottage.

"Merry Christmas, Sis," Maddox replies, leaning in, he kisses his sister on the cheek.

"Merry Christmas, Sab," I echo.

My best friend just stands there, looking at the two of us. "You gonna let us in? It's cold enough to freeze the balls off a brass monkey out here."

"Ohhh, yeah, come on in."

We step inside and Maddox takes off his coat and then helps me with mine. We shuffle the presents and dessert between us and once we're coat and snow boot free, he slides his hand into mine. Sab squeals, she literally squeals and covers her mouth, jumping up and down with excitement. The last time I saw her this excited was when we got tickets to see OneRepublic.

Mad and I both stop and stare—sorry, bad OneRepublic song pun—at my crazy best friend.

"You right there, Sis?" Maddox asks her.

"It's just, I always wanted you two together and look, it's a Christmas miracle."

It's funny, when she said she was over the moon for us the other day I just thought she was being nice after the Joel debacle, but seeing her reaction in the flesh, I know she means it. She is genuinely happy Mad and I are together.

"Well, you kinda have that ornament to thank," I tell her.

"I knew it was magical," she beams. It's almost as if she wants to take credit for all of this happening between Mad and me, but in reality, it's because of Joel ditching me at the altar. I do wish he'd done it in a less public way but from what I heard, the party was a good one.

"You didn't know shit," Mad scoffs.

"You said a naughty word, Uncle Mad," Cassie sings out from the other room, her supersonic hearing once again getting me into trouble. "That's a dollar for the swear jar."

"At this rate, her college will be paid for before the holidays are over," Eamon says, joining us in the entryway. He shakes Mad's hand and pulls me in for a one-armed hug.

"Who's got the potty mouth this year?"

"Dad," Sabrina says with a laugh. "It's like since he's stopped working his brain to mouth filter retired too, and he just says what he wants. As much as it's bad for the girls, it's highly entertaining."

As is the fact, for the last few days, Sab has been trapped with her parents, husband, and her two munchkins in this cottage ... while I was trapped with her brother. I think I had the better deal. She seems to be coping well but that thought is quashed when she says, "Who wants a margarita?"

Everyone says yes, so we move the party from the entryway and head into the living area. Mad and I say hello to his parents and then I help Sab with the drinks. We make virgin margs for the girls and extra strong ones for the adults.

The eight of us have a wonderful afternoon together eating yummy Christmas foods, opening presents, and laughing. Oh my God, do we laugh. I have to say, it's one of the best Christmas's I've had in a long time.

By the time Mad and I get back to my place, later that evening, we are full of yummy food and ready to call it a night. We were going to go back to his place since he has food and I don't. I was supposed to be on my honeymoon right now, hence the bare fridge and pantry. We're both exhausted so we decide to stay here.

Stripping off because sleeping naked is much more fun, Mad and I climb into bed and snuggle together. My body fits up against his perfectly. Lifting my head up, I stare at him. He looks down and smiles at me. Reaching up, I cup his cheek in my palm and run the pad of my finger over his lips. He nips and kisses my fingertip before covering my hand on his cheek.

"I love you," he mouths, and I mouth the sentiment back. I may have been left at the altar a few days ago, but my life isn't over. It's just beginning because this right here, it feels right. This is where I'm meant to be, and Maddox is "the one."

Just like my Christmas ornament predicted.

thirty-eight

MADDOX

IT'S the day before New Year's Eve, the second to last day of what has turned out to be a pretty good year. I got my dream job as Sheriff of Evergreen Lake. It meant returning to the small town I grew up in but it also led me back to her, Ruby "Reindeer" Olsen. Sure, when I got here she was engaged to another man but he fucked that up—thank you, Joel—and thanks to the magic of Christmas, I can finally call the woman of my dreams mine. Tomorrow night, we're having our first official real date and I have something up my sleeve, but first, we are spending the afternoon ice-skating and drinking hot chocolate. This doesn't count as our first date, it's just an afternoon of fun that's kinda like a date.

Hand in hand, Reindeer and I skate around and around the ice rink. Her blond hair flies behind her, even with her purple beanie pulled low on her head, she looks cute. She looks cute in everything she wears but that beanie of hers makes her extra cute because it makes her hazel eyes glow.

Dropping my hand, she skates ahead and I take a moment to just watch her. She's so carefree right now. She's smiling brightly, I don't think I have ever seen her so happy. Catching up to her, I take her hand in mine again and tug on her hand, causing us to stop in the middle of the rink. Pulling her to me, I slide my arm around her waist. "You know, I always wanted to bring you here."

"We should make it a tradition. On the second last day of the year, we will go ice-skating and follow it up with hot chocolate before you take me home and—"

Leaning into her, I whisper, "Fuck you in the ass."

She slaps me on the chest and shakes her head. "Oh my God, you're addicted."

"Yep, have you seen your ass?" And for emphasis, I squeeze her ass.

"I was going to say, you can take me home and cook me chicken Alfredo"—she leans into me and huskily murmurs in my ear—"and then fuck me in the ass."

"I knew I loved you for a reason." There are so many reasons why I love this woman, and I will remind her each and every time that I do. I've never felt so deeply about someone before, and I think that's because she's always been the one for me.

"It better be for more than just f-u-c-k-i-n-g my a-s-s." She spells the naughty words because a few little kids are in earshot right now.

"You know it is but that's in the top five of my fave things about Ruby Olsen."

"And what might be on this top five list of yours?"

"You really want to know?" She nods. "Okay, well, number one, your heart. It's bigger than my coc—ego." She chuckles and the sound is music to my ears. "You'd do anything for those around you, even if it put you at a disadvantage. Two, you're adventurous and open to new and crazy adventures."

"Like skinny-dipping in December with your sister," she reminds me, and it's my turn to laugh.

"Yes, things like that. Three, you took a gamble and opened a bookstore with a wine bar in a small town."

"I did do that and it's the best decision I ever made. I know it's not using my English Lit degree to its fullest potential, but I love what I do."

"I know you do and it shows because Read Between the Wines is thriving."

"What's number four?"

"Your a-s-s, which I don't need to elaborate on but just to be safe, I better have a squeeze and yes, it's still fine and I can't wait to get up close and personal with it later tonight."

"Fiend," she teases.

"Yet you still love me.

"That I do, Maddox. That I do."

"And that brings me to five, you love me unconditionally and just as much as I love you. I never thought I'd get a second chance with you, but Fate had other plans for us. Now that I have my shot, I'm not taking it or you for granted. You're it for me, Ruby Olsen." I might be coming on a little strong right now but I want nothing but honesty between us. She and Joel weren't honest with one another and they nearly got married. When I marry Ruby, and I will, I want there to be no doubt from either one of us when we say our "I dos" to one another.

She just stands there, staring at me. Her eyes are primed with tears and one falls over the edge, reaching out, I wipe it away. "Mad, you and I have the same top five but in place of my career in number three, yours would be for following your heart to the academy and achieving your dream of becoming sheriff."

She lifts her hands, cups my cheeks in her palms, and presses her lips to mine. "I'm so happy you came back to town."

"Me too, Reindeer, me too ... now let's go home and I'll—"

"Fuck me in the ass?" A mother skating by gasps in shock,

causing Reindeer's eyes to widen and for me to chuckle. She slaps me in the chest, and it causes me to laugh harder.

"I can do that but I was going to say, I need to feed you ... because you'll need sustenance for what I have planned tonight."

thirty-nine

RUBY

I'M TECHNICALLY STILL on leave but being at home with nothing to do is making me go crazy. I can only clean my place, or Maddox's, so many times before I'll start to take the varnish off of things. And there's no more room in my freezer thanks to all the cooking and baking I've done.

Speaking of baking, a cake is cooling on the counter but that one is for the guys down at the station, I decided to bake them a treat, and who can pass up a slice of homemade chocolate fudge cake? Exactly, no one.

Stopping in at Sips, I walk up to the counter and order coffees for each of the guys and myself. Taking a seat, I pull out my phone but before I can start mindlessly scrolling Facebook, I feel a presence behind me. Looking over my shoulder, I smile when I see Mildred, Bernice, and Shelia all crowded around me. "Good morning, ladies."

"Good morning, Ruby," comes from them and it sounds like when first graders say good morning to their teacher, but no sooner have they finished their hello and Mildred blurts out, "You're better off without that boy." Her tone is curt and she means business.

"Yep, you deserve someone who will rub your feet after a long day at your book shop but most of all you deserve someone who won't leave you at the altar. What sort of man does that?" Bernice says shaking her head. "I'll tell you who, a no-good, spineless raccoon. That's who." Bernice goes on and on, telling us all what she really thought about Joel.

And not wanting to be left out, Sheila interrupts Bernice's rant and adds her two cents as well. "Never did like that buffoon, his beady eyes gave way to his true nature. Like Mildred said, you're better off without him."

Shaking my head, I turn around to face them. "Ladies, Joel is not the bad guy here, yes, he stood me up but really, we're both at fault because we didn't talk to one another. This is why communication is key in any relationship. If Joel and I had been honest with each other, it would have ended differently."

The three of them nod in agreement, suddenly changing their tune and opinion of Joel. We all know how much these three love to "communicate," even if it's by spreading rumors and gossip around town.

"Speaking of communication," Mildred changes the subject. "If the latest gossip I hear is true, Deputy Drew went skinny-dipping with two women." I chuckle at that. I mean yes, he was there while two women—me and Sab—were skinny-dipping, but he wasn't with them-with them, but before I can correct her, she swivels her finger around in my face. "And rumor has it, you rode out the storm last week with our new sheriff and you were seen on a date yesterday ice-skating wi—"

"Well, I heard," Bernice interrupts, "tonight, you two are going out on another date and Sheriff Whi—"

"Don't you think it's too soon to be dating?" Sheila butts in, disdain written all over her face.

Thankfully, I don't have to answer because Sydney arrives with my tray of coffees. She places them on the counter and turns her gaze to the G-team. "At the end of the day, ladies, as long as Rubes is happy and no one is breaking any laws, then that's all that matters when it comes to love and the heart."

"And it's none of our business," Mildred throws out there.

Sydney and I can't help but chuckle, she was the one to bring up the gossip about Mad and me. Out of nowhere, she pulls me into a hug and whispers, "Your pop would be happy you and our sheriff are together."

A smile appears on my face because I know she's right. Like Sab, Pop always hoped I'd end up with Maddox and like usual, I should have listened to the wise old man.

While I was thinking about Pop, the G-team has turned their focus away from me and are now questioning Sydney about her and Dennis.

As much as I'd love to stay and get the gossip there, I'm going to make my escape while I can. With a wave, I grab the tray of coffees and head out to my car. Putting it into gear, I pull out onto Evergreen Drive and make my way around to the station. When I arrive, I somehow manage to balance the coffees and the cake container in my hands without dropping them, and I make my way into the station.

Walking up to the counter, I notice the front area is empty. Placing the coffees and cake down on the counter, I lean over and sing out, "Hello?" I'm met with silence. "Hmmmpf, where could they be?"

I'm just about to call Mad when a door in the back slams and then Dennis rushes in. When he sees me, he stops, looking all sheepish. "Ruby, what are you doing here?" I notice that he shouted my name loud. He's being weird, even for Dennis. He's always been a little quirky but this is next level weird.

"I brought coffees and I baked a cake." He mutely stares at me. "What are you up to back there?"

"Nothing," he refutes, but his tone is three octaves higher than normal.

"Oooookay, is the sheriff in?" He nods but doesn't move. "You wanna get him for me?" Again he nods but he doesn't move an inch, and then the man in question returns with Drew close behind him. When he sees me, his face lights up like a Christmas tree. "Reindeer, what are you doing here?"

"She brought us coffee and cake," Dennis answers for me.

"Your famous chocolate fudge one?" Drew excitedly asks and when I nod, he fist pumps the air and hisses a, "Yesss."

"You guys enjoy the cake, I'm gonna take my girl out for lunch," Maddox says and at the prospect of me not being here any longer, Dennis visibly relaxes. *What's going on?*

"I'd love that," I tell him with a smile.

"Give me a sec." Without waiting for me to answer, he walks into his office. Dennis and Drew scurry after him, I can hear murmuring but I can't make out what they are saying. The three of them are definitely up to something but then again, they're the law, maybe they're dealing with a sensitive case or something.

A few moments later, they all return. Dennis and Drew go straight for the coffee and cake, while Mad walks around the counter and over to me. "Let's go," he singsongs as he joins me. Placing his hand on my lower back, he escorts me out of the station.

Lacing my fingers with his, we stroll over to the main street and make our way around to Hips and Lips. I'm craving Norah's delicious chicken noodle soup. We're just passing Gingerbreads when Maddox stops suddenly. Looking up, my eyes widen when I realize why he stopped.

"Joel," I screech, not expecting to see him before us. I quickly drop Mad's hand like I've been caught out, but it's silly because I haven't been caught doing anything. I'm literally walking down the street to get lunch with my boyfriend, my new boyfriend. I mean, it's not like there's an etiquette for when you run into your ex who dumped you at the altar the week before and you're with your new boyfriend.

"Hey, Ruby," Joel says as he stops before Maddox and me. "How are you?"

"I'm ... I'm good, you?"

"I'm good too."

A silence envelops the three of us. It's awkward and when I look around, my gaze lands on Sips and I see three faces pressed to the front window. Shaking my head, I chuckle. "What's so funny?" Mad asks.

"We have an audience," I tell him and discreetly nod my head toward Sips.

Not so discreetly, both Mad and Joel turn their heads in the direction I nodded, *men*. "Ohh, ummm, is there somewhere we can talk?" Joel rushes out. "Maybe in private."

"My wine bar? It's a Tuesday so it shouldn't be too busy."

"Yep, yeah, sure, okay," Joel awkwardly agrees.

"I'm gonna head back to the station," Maddox says.

"Actually," Joel says, "I'd like to talk to both of you."

Joel's statement shocks me. "Really?" He nods.

I look to Maddox and he just shrugs, "Well, ummm, okay, then."

"Shall we?" I offer and then I put my head down and race across the road and over to the store.

The bell overhead rings and from the back, Charlene calls out, "I'll just be a minute."

"It's just me," I sing back. "Joel, Mad, and I—"

"I thought you just said Jo—" Her words die on her lips when she sees the three of us standing in the entrance.

"Ohh, ummm, hiiiii ... everyone." Her gaze flicks between the three of us.

"We're just going to talk in there," I point to the other room.

She begins to nod. "Oooookay, I'll just." She flicks behind her and heads to the back office without saying anything else. Tuesdays are delivery days so I know she has stock to check off and organize. Charlene is a stickler for organization and she'll be in seventh heaven right now ... while I'm in the depths of hell about to chat with my ex-fiancé and my current boyfriend.

"Well, this is awkward," I mumble, and without acknowledging the guys, I walk into the bar area and behind the counter. They follow and each take a seat at the bar. Grabbing a bottle of red, I pour a glass and quickly chug it back. Then I grab two more glasses, I refill mine and then fill theirs before handing them out.

"I'm on duty," Maddox informs me and Joel says, "I'm driving,"

"Riiight," I nervously draw the word out. Taking another sip, I look over the rim of my glass at Joel. Swallowing my mouthful, I place the glass down. "You wanted to talk?"

"I ... I wanted to apologize to you, Ruby. I shouldn't have done that to you, and I will forever be sorry for how I behaved."

"That's nice of you, Joel, and I appreciate the apology, but why did you leave it till the last minute?" Over the past week, I've rehashed every moment and looking back at the lead-up to the wedding, he was clearly having doubts then. He was always absent and "working" and everything was left for me to do. Hell, Maddox helped me with the thank-yous and a few other last-minute wedding items. It should have been my fiancé helping me with those, not another man.

"Because I'm gutless," he dejectedly utters. "When I proposed, I honestly wanted to marry you but the closer our big day got, the more I started to fear the future. But at the same time, I wanted you to be happy but when I woke up that morning, I just knew I couldn't go through with it. I ... I couldn't put your happiness above mine an—"

"But you waited till right before the ceremony to tell me, why didn't you do it as soon as you knew?"

"I ... I don't know, and I will always regret doing that but seeing you so happy now, I know I made the right choice."

"When did you see me happy?"

"Yesterday," he says. "I came here to talk to you but when you weren't here, I went for a walk around the square and then on my way back to check here again, I saw the two of you at the ice skating rink. I haven't seen you smile like that in a very long-time, Ruby." He stops and looks thoughtful at the memory he's recalling. "You threw your head back and laughed, a proper belly laugh, and when I saw that, I knew I'd made the right choice, but at the same time, I was gutted I no longer had that. Which is stupid because I'm the one who walked away."

Another silence befalls us but it's broken when Maddox speaks. "I have a question for you, Joel." *Ohh shit,* I think to myself, *this can't be good.* "Why did you come to the station and ream me out that day?"

"To be honest, I'm not entirely sure. I had a feeling you cared deeply for her, and I guess I wanted you to confirm my suspicion. Maybe even find out she was cheating so I could end it without remorse, but after chatting with you, I knew you weren't together but I think I always knew that." He looks intently at me. "You'd never cheat, I know that now but at that point, I ... I was struggling with what I wanted. I think, deep down, I wanted to make sure if I decided to leave Ruby that she'd have support."

"And you didn't think I cared for her?"

"Looking back now, I know you did, but at the time, I wasn't confident. I couldn't break her heart if she had no one, so I decided to suck it up and marry her."

"Joel," I cry, "your happiness matters too."

"I know that, and that's why I did what I did."

"I just wish you'd told me, Joel. We always said, communication is key."

"I know, but be honest, you moved on pretty quickly, which tells me you too had doubts." I go to interrupt but he raises his hand. "I'm not angry about that, I'm just stating we we're both at fault."

He's right; we're both to blame. Neither one of us said anything, we just kept going along as if everything was fine. Imagine if we had gotten married, it would have been a divorce just waiting to happen. "You're right, Joel. I'm sorry."

"What's done is done, Ruby. No need for apologies but I really am happy that you're happy."

"I hope you find happiness one of these days too, Joel."

"I'm sure I will."

Walking out from behind the bar, I hug Joel one last time and slip off the engagement ring I've still been wearing, and I hand it to him. Being the gentleman he is, he tries to give it back to me but I refuse. Eventually, he takes it and with nothing else left to say, he walks out of my life.

Standing here, I stare after him, feeling lighter after our conversation. Maddox steps behind me and wraps his arms around my waist, I lean back into him and his support means everything to me. "You okay?"

"Yeah, I think I am." Looking over my shoulder at him, I ask a question I'm not sure I want the answer to, "Do you think he'll be okay?"

"I really do," he confirms with a nod. "He was just lost and confused. Yes, he made a mistake but then again, sounds like you both did."

"Yeah, we both did."

Turning in his arms, I drape mine over his shoulders. "Thank you for being here for that."

"I'll always be here, Reindeer. Anywhere, anytime. Now, let's get you home so you can change. Rumor has it, you and I have a date tonight."

"That we do, and just so you know," I lean into him and whisper, "I put out on the first date."

forty
MADDOX

SITTING on the end of the bed, I'm a Nervous Nelly. My palms are sweaty and my heart is racing. *Is this what a heart attack feels like?* I'm in my jeans and purple Henley. Reindeer is in the bathroom, right now she's all soapy and wet, I couldn't be in there with her because I'd cave and I can't ruin this.

The shower turns off and that somehow makes me even more nervous because it means we are one step closer to getting to the fair and my surprise.

Slipping my feet into my boots, I sit back up and stare at the wall. I don't know why I'm so nervous. Reindeer and I have been to the fair together plenty of times, but this will be the first time as a couple. A real couple.

"Mad, babe, you okay?" The sounds of her voice causes me to yelp and jump. Turning my head toward her, my eyes bug out of my head when I see her standing in the doorway in a deep purple bra and panty set. "Fuck, babe, you're stunning."

She smiles and then she spins around and shows me her delectable ass. "Fuck it," I growl. Standing up, I walk over to her and take her hands in mine. "Reindeer, I know you just ended an engagement but when you know, you know and, Ruby

Olsen, I love you to the moon and back. I've loved you since you were a teenager and I would be honored if you'd be my wife. So, what do you say, will you marry me, Reindeer?"

She blankly stares at me, she doesn't blink and she doesn't utter a word. Not one peep and I'm almost positive she's stopped breathing. Then her head starts to bob up and down. "Y-y-yes," she stammers, then she clears her throat and lets out a husky, "Yes, Mad, I'll marry you." She's smiling like a carnival clown, and I'm pretty sure my face mirrors hers right now.

"The ring," I scoff, reaching into the side table. I dig to the back and grab the velvet box. Opening it, I take out the ring, a pear-shaped ruby flanked by round and marquise diamonds. I slide it onto her finger and just like her to me, it fits perfectly.

I want to shout, *"She said yes!"* for the world to hear, but there's no one here but the two of us. I was a little eager and I did it before we got to the fair. Dennis and Drew are gonna be pissed I ruined our hard work, but seeing the smile on her face right now, I don't really care about them and their feelings.

She admires her hand, the light from behind her in the en suite reflects off the ruby and diamond, and she's smiling just as bright as the gems on her finger. She lifts her head and stares seductively at me. "Do we really have to go tonight? I'm suddenly not in the mood to go out ... and I have a new jar of coconut oil, we can celebrate our engagement, just the two of us." She winks at me, and my cock springs to life in my jeans.

"As much as I love that plan, we really need to go, because I kinda had this amazing romantic proposal organized. Dennis and Drew will be pissed if we don't turn up."

"Is that what you three were colluding about yesterday?"

"Yep. You arrived with coffee and cake when the jeweler was there. Drew knew someone who knew someone and she came by the station, coming in through the back so no one would know. She'd just left when you arrived but the ring was still sitting on the counter in the back."

"You're lucky I didn't just barge in, otherwise, the surprise would have been ruined … But then again, you kinda ruined the surprise by proposing now and not waiting to do it at the fair, but to be honest, I'm glad we did it like this … even if I am half naked."

"So what you're saying is we need to go to the fair and have a public, suitable for work proposal?"

The plan was for me to do it tonight at the fair on the carousel. Dennis was going to Nadine's Nursery to pick up a bouquet of her favorite flowers, peonies, and because I'm a corny bastard, I got a dozen *ruby*-red roses too. The ring was going to be sitting in one of the flowers and they would be hidden on the carousel near the Christmas wagon. Reindeer and I were going to hop on. and I would propose when the lights dimmed and the music stopped.

"Yes … plus we wouldn't want to upset Drew and Dennis. Dennis is already surly enough over his Syd drama, and I hate seeing him down."

"Like us, I'm sure they'll get their shit together, after all, love is in the air."

Reindeer gets dressed—boo—and then we head to the fair. She gives me the ring back and in front of all of our friends, I propose for a second time, on the carousel like I had planned.

The other day I said this year was pretty good, but now I can unequivocally say, it's the best fucking year ever. My luck started to turn when I was on my way back into town and I found the Christmas ornament that led me to "the one."

Happy fucking New Year to me!

epilogue

RUBY

...TWELVE MONTHS *later*

Today, just like I always dreamed, is the day Maddox and I become husband and wife, and Sab will officially be my sister from another mister.

The ceremony and reception is being held in a tent with gas heaters to keep the guests warm and a clear back that overlooks the lake. Yep, I'm finally getting my Christmas lakeside wedding.

The twinkling lights of the houses along the shoreline sparkle in the background as Maddox and I say our vows in front of our family and friends. We had to move the ceremony inside due to an impending snowstorm but to be honest, as long as I became Mad's wife, I really didn't care where it happened. Hell, I would have done it at the courthouse but I am glad we get to do it here.

"Maddox, I've been in love with you for as long as I can remember. You were my first crush, my first everything, and now, you're my one and only but thanks to a magical Christmas ornament—"

"And me," Sab interrupts, causing everyone to laugh.

"As I was saying, thanks to a magical Christmas ornament, and Sab, we found each other again. Now that you're mine, I'm never letting you go. You are my everything, Maddox Whitworth, and I cannot wait to spend the rest of my life with you."

"Reindeer, I stupidly let you get away when you were nineteen, but it seems Fate had a plan for us all along because we are here today, declaring our love for one another in front of all our family and friends. Coming back to Evergreen Lake was the best decision, both professionally and personally. It led me back to the best thing to ever come into my life." He raises his hand and points at his sister. "And no, Sis, it's not because you are her best friend and met her first. Like she said, Fate had a plan for us and no matter what, we would have met ... and with the help of a little Christmas magic. I love you, Reindeer, and I will do so for the rest of my life and into eternity and beyond."

After his beautiful vows, I've never been so eager to utter those two magical words, I do! And as soon as they pass through my lips and he slips that ring onto my finger, I know, no matter what happens from here on out, it will all be fine. With Maddox by my side, we can conquer anything.

Finally, I get to kiss my husband and like our first kiss when we rekindled our romance just over twelve months ago, my leg lifts AND my heart skips a beat. Just like the heroines in the books I sell, I got the man and my happily ever after.

After a million and one photos, waiters begin delivering delicious finger foods. The bar staff keep the bubbly flowing and the DJ plays upbeat music with the odd romantic song thrown in, it is a wedding after all.

The day is perfect in every way, just like my husband.

Maddox Whitworth has owned my heart since I was a teenager, back then I was hopelessly in love with him and now that I'm an adult, hopelessly in love is an understatement. He's the only one to ever truly get under my skin, or in my ass. My husband is literally the man of my dreams, and now, I get to grow old with my one true love.

Sab still maintains it's because of her and the guidance of a magical Christmas ornament that led us to our happily ever after, but personally, I think Maddox and I were always destined to be together.

In the middle of the dance floor, I sway in my husband's arms. I'm officially Mrs. Maddox Whitworth, and my life is complete. I got the fairy-tale ending and in nine months' time, our family will be expanding—but shh, that's *my* Christmas present for my husband.

Merry freaking Christmas to me!

THE END!

Ready for the next book in the Evergreen Lake: Under the Mistletoe series? Check out The Write Before Christmas by Lynessa Layne.

Holiday in Handcuffs

Sprinkle All The Way

Hung by the Fire

Tangled with the Tight End

Winter Falls

The Christmas Ornament

The Write Before Christmas

Mistletoe Magic

Jingle Balls

Deer in Headlights - Sia
Dear Future Husband - Meghan Trainor
Teenage Dream - Katy Perry
True Love - P!nk, feat. Lily Allen
Christmas Lights - Coldplay
Last Christmas - Wham!
Winter Wonderland - Blake Shelton
Me And My Broken Heart - Rixton
Tear You Better - Shawn Mendes
Santa Tell Me - Ariana Grande
Driving Home for Christmas - Chris Rea
Rockin' Around the Christmas Tree - Brenda Lee
I Want It That Way - Backstreet Boys
Closer - Nine Inch Nails
Wildest Dreams - Taylor Swift
Stitches - Shawn Mendes
One Last Time - Ariana Grande
Just the Way You Are - Bruno Mars
Grenade - Bruno Mars
Bang Bang - Jessies J, Ariana Grande, Nicki Minaj

A Sky Full of Stars - Coldplay
Bad Day - Daniel Potter
2002 - Anne-Marie
Something Just Like This - The Chainsmokers, Coldplay
Wake Me Up - Avicii
Say You Won't Let Go - James Arthur
Dusk Till Dawn - ZAYN feat. Sia
Waiting For Love _ Avicii
Into Dust - Mazzy Star
Blank Space - Taylor Swift
Hey, Soul Sister - Train
Demons - Imagine Dragons
Burn - Ellie Goulding
Fight Song - Rachel Platten
Sorry - Justin Beiber
Rudolph The Red-Nosed Reindeer - Dean Martin
There's Nothing Holdin' Me Back - Shawn Mendes
Wolves - Selena Gomez, Marshmello
What Makes You Beautiful - One Direction
I Don't Wanna Wait - David Guetta, OneRepublic
Stop And Stare - OneRepublic

The playlist can be found on Spotify.

acknowledgments

These things never get any easier and I always feel like I've forgotten someone so this is a blanket *thank you* to everyone who I have crossed paths with on this authoring journey over the last 8 years.

First and foremost, I need to thank **Nicole Sanchez** for inviting me to me a part of the Evergreen Lake collection. I loved writing this story and without you, Ruby and Maddox would never have been created.

To my fellow Evergreen Lake authors; **Nicole Sanchez, Kayla Martin, Shea Brighton, Alexia Chase, Shana Gray, Lynessa Layne, Rebecca Barber** and **Rhian Cahill**, thank you for the fun times and amazing stories. I have loved each and every one I've read and really wish that Evergreen Lake was a real place.

Karen Hrdlicka from **Barren Acres Editing**; thank you for everything that you do for me. You are not only my editor but you are a dear friend too.

Victoria, thank you for checking all my I's are dotted, my T's are crossed, there's no extra e's or s's and repetitive words. Ohh, and for the kickass blurb, you nailed it and I think this is my most fav blurb of mine.

Jordan, thank you for the cover. It's stunning by itself but lined up with the other eight books, it's amazeballs. You outdid yourself, thank you.

My beta babes **Bec, Rhi Rhi, Margaret and Sarah;** I would be lost without you ladies. You give me advice when I second guess everything and you helped bring this story to life. Thank you from the bottom of my heart.

Troy, my husband, my everything. You really are awesome at what you do and you're an even better husband and father. Love you long-time dude.

To my munchkins, **Piper** and **Kade**. You two are my greatest achievement and I'm so lucky to have you both in my life. Love you long-time guys and I look forward to the day when you are forty and can finally read my books.

And finally, **you, my reader**. Thanks for taking a chance on this holiday story. I hope you love Rubes and Maddox as much as I do.

Cheers,

Dana XoXoX

STAND ALONES

Antecedent

Doc Steel

Oops

Off the Books

Out of Nowhere

Deck...the Balls

Secrets and Sunrises

Always in the Cards

Fractured

The Christmas Ornament

Before the Ashes

After the Ashes

Love Me Like You Do

Never Let Me Go

Seven Nights

Seven Kisses

PUCKING LOVE SERIES

I Pucking Hate That I Love You

A Pucking Good Christmas

I Pucking Hate That You Love Me

I Pucking Hate To Love You

It's Pucking Fake

...and a few pucking more

FALLING NOVELS

These men make it hard not to fall for them

Falling for Dr. Kelly

Falling for Dr. Knight

Falling for Agent Cox

Falling for Agent Cruz

Falling:The Complete Collection

LORDS OF CRESTWOOD PREP

Co-write with Tara Lee

Thatcher

Reign

Hendrix

Saint

THE UNEXPECTED SERIES

When it comes to love, expect the unexpected

The Unexpected Gift

The Unexpected Letter

The Unexpected Package

The Unexpected Connection

The Unexpected series: The Complete Collection

THE LIQUOR CABINET SERIES

Liquor has never been so disturbingly saucy

Malt Me (Book 1)

Tequila Healing (Book 2)

Wine Not (Book 3)

The Final Shot (Book 4)

The Liquor Cabinet: Series boxset

All of these books are available on Amazon.

DL Gallie is from Queensland, Australia, but she's lived in many different places all over the world, including the UK and Canada. She currently resides in Central Queensland with her husband and two munchkins. She and her husband have been together since she was sixteen, and although they drive each other crazy at times, she couldn't imagine her life without him.

Shortly after her son was born, DL began reading again. With encouragement from her husband, she picked up the pen and started writing, and now the voices in her head won't shut up.

DL enjoys listening to music, drinking white wine in the summer, red wine in the winter, and beer all year round. She's also never been known to turn down a cocktail, especially a margarita.